OZ

HOPE SWAN

Illustrator/Cover Artist: Matthew Broughton

Editing by Tara Jean

Formatted by Flutterby Formatting

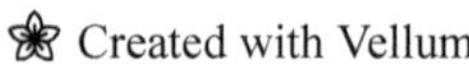

This is for Mickey. I love you forever.

CONTENT WARNING

Swearing / Violence / Insinuation of sex being used as payment for things / Sexual assault (unwanted grabbing and some bad language)

Please contact me for a list of specific pages etc to avoid. (I'm happy to quickly summarise what happens so you can still read the book and not be triggered!)

Dorothy is gone, and Oz is in shambles.

Delia sits at home and wishes for an exciting life.

She is the only one who can save Oz from the reign of the Wizard.

She just doesn't know it yet.

PROLOGUE

Oz has been around for generations; we've all heard of it. The mystical land with monkeys and Munchkins where Dorothy 'found' herself. The little girl that came along and defeated the wickedest of witches and saved us all. It's real. Oh god, is it real. Just not like everyone believes. There are some... how should I put this?

Discrepancies.

Dorothy came to Oz from Kansas?

Check.

Dorothy defeated the Wicked Witch?

Check.

Dorothy woke up in her bed in Kansas, Oz and her new friends seemingly a dream?

Nope.

Dorothy saved Oz, and in the meantime, gained a lot of fans. Everyone was so grateful to the little girl. They wanted her to lead. She couldn't, of course, being underage and all but asked her friend the Cowardly Lion to do so on her behalf.

When she came of age, she became one of Oz's most beloved figure heads, the terror and the poverty induced by the reign of the

Witch almost completely gone. More Ozians enrolled their children in school than ever. The arts sector began to thrive, agriculture became popular once more and laughter returned to the streets of the Emerald City.

And not just there, but in all of Oz.

For years, Dorothy ruled into her middle age. She would swear she did nothing different to what any good ruler would do, but the citizens would swear she was a godsend. Oz was once again the place of myth, so wonderful that anyone outside of it would not believe it.

We don’t know what happened to her. Just that one day she was here, and the next?

Gone.

CHAPTER ONE

The changes throughout Oz once Dorothy disappeared were quick.

More people locked their doors.

Children began dropping out of school.

On the third day, flyers were up in every corner of Oz. From the Emerald City to Munchkin Land, purple signs were tacked on every spare bit of space. They declared the arrival of the Wizard's Coalition and the new ruler of Oz, Marcus Rightfoot.

The Coalition's main argument was that as the most "powerful" beings in Oz, they were the most equipped to take over from Dorothy. They claimed that Rightfoot, as their leader, was the best of them. This quickly became not the case. A strong guard was installed instantly, one that all around Oz could enforce every belief of not just Rightfoot but the Wizards as a whole. Many guards grew to resent Marcus after a few years, Ozian's threatening their lives as they enforced the archaic rules.

Marcus's first rule, however, began simply.

He was to be known as the 'Great Wizard of Oz.'

It was from there that everything got serious.

They murdered Munchkins for saying the wrong things. Winkies were to be shot on sight if found outside after dark. And the witches? We're told that if they used witch magic, they would be publicly executed.

We start our story in the ruby red streets of the South Country. Only they weren't looking so red anymore.

Buildings covered in dirt and grime, Quadlings darting back and forth, no one daring to look up from their commute. The clothes of all citizens, ripped and ruined, dirtied and decimated by time. Many shiver as their clothes no longer provide the warmth they need. Figures are malnourished and guards march down the street in steady intervals. A man breaks the monotony of the crowd, walking dazed, arms clutched around his torso. He eyes the approaching round of guards, then launches himself at their feet. The group of guards stops moving.

"I haven't eaten in days. My wife is dead and my daughter will soon follow. Her bones–I can see them all. She doesn't laugh or play anymore. She doesn't smile. Her cough will haunt me forever."

The guard directly in front of the man does not move. The helmet, hard and unforgiving, no sign of any expression underneath. Tightening his grip on the guard's slacks, the man continues.

"You're killing us. You're all killing us. Why does the Wizard hate us so?"

Sobbing, the man looks up at the guard.

Kicking his leg, the guard watches the man tumble to the ground, dirt flying. "The Wizard does not care about your insignificant problems, your miniature complaints. Leave or we will arrest you."

The crowd that had been hurrying by formed a loose circle around the guards, each carefully and curiously watching the communication between the two.

The man lunges forward, pulling a knife from the back of his pants, aiming at the guard's throat. Before anything can happen, a loud shot rings out across the street. The man falls in slow motion, back towards the ground, a large red spot blossoming on his chest. The guards part, revealing another guard holding a gun.

Identical to the others but oozing confidence, this guard clearly holds a position of authority. He slowly approaches the body, gaze focused on the man that he has killed and kneels over him, like he was mourning. After a moment, the guard stands, reaching around the back of his head and pulls off his helmet, revealing a middle-aged man with sparkling blue eyes.

"See what happens? You all know how you are meant to act! The Wizards are here now. Dorothy is gone." His roaring can be heard from streets away, and the crowd that had gathered to watch the interaction between the Quadling man and the guard had well and truly dispersed at this point.

Other guards step forward and begin dragging the body away. It's scary how quickly the streets go back to the way they were before. The dead man may as well have never existed.

The next place of importance in our tale is the "Emerald Tavern." A bar that sits just on the outside of the Emerald City. Throughout the reign of the Wicked Witch and the introduction of the Wizard and his Coalition, the Tavern has been a popular spot where factions from all over Oz find solace.

'Bustling' is the only way to describe the Tavern on this night. Two ogres sit at the bar, knocking back pints of beer the size of the pixie serving them. Citizens scattered official Emerald City clothing all over the bar, too scared to be seen wearing anything that breaks the official dress code. The citizens are relaxed, as relaxed as you will find, gripping their drinks like they are the lifeline out of their nightmare. A hooded figure sits off in a booth alone, nursing a drink. Three off duty guards sit at a table close to the bar, identifiable by the helmets sitting in amongst the used pitchers.

Suddenly the bar falls quiet.

The doorknob to the tavern twists, and the door flies open, intoxicated laughs ringing through the silent bar. Three men walk through the door, each wearing an overcoat of bright colour and shiny silver boots. The first man through the door flicks his wrist and nearly every worker in the bar rushes towards them, clearly eager to attend to their every need. A tall man with a large beard ushers them behind a cornered off VIP area. The man nods towards a young barmaid, who scurries forward towards the wizards. Shaking, the young girl writes their orders.

"What do I get for a bit extra?"

"Do you come with the package?"

"I'm sure I could make it good for you."

They all laugh, one pushing her towards the bar, hand a little too low down the back. The tall man, that led the wizards in, watches, cleaning a glass. His grip tightens, but he doesn't step forward to intervene.

Slowly, the sound of the bar from before returned, as the Ozians within breathe a sigh of relief that the wizards' attention was not directed at them.

The figure at the booth had been watching the whole thing unfold. Watching as the girl brought out their drinks and the wizard in a purple coat grabs her chest. The watching figure holds back a sob, clearly mortified, as the girl is unable to move.

Beginning to shift uncomfortably, the figure grows further distressed by how the girl is being treated. Putting down the drink, the figure raises a finger toward the group.

The drinks that had been just placed down lurched up, a stream of beer flying up into the faces of the wizards, drenching them from head to toe.

Standing up, the men draw the attention of the bar's patrons once more.

"This is witch magic," the one in the purple coat declares, to no one really in particular.

The wizard in an orange coat turns to the barmaid, who had only just made it back to the safety of behind the bar.

"You? Was it you, you stupid bitch?"

In the meantime, the third wizard has flicked their hand, slamming the door shut.

"No one leaves!"

Murmurs filter back and forth from all around the bar. The figure, who has been sitting simply watching everything happen, tilts their head back slowly, their hood falling away to reveal striking green eyes and blonde hair. The wizards have walked around inspecting the patrons of the bar. The one wearing a yellow coat meets the figure's eyes.

"You..."

The woman smirks.

The wizard lunges towards the mysterious woman, arms reaching for her neck, but before he can reach her, she is gone.

Disappeared.

Now we visit the North Country. Home to the proud Gilikin people. Like the roads of South Country, North Country has darkened. The gleaming violet that the city was once famous for? Gone. Replaced with a dirtied and horrifying land that no one could recognise.

. . .

Three women walk together down the main street of Gilikin Country. All are wearing long coats, hoods thrown haphazardly over their heads. Their laughter stands out against the quiet. One woman threw back her hood with a particularly loud laugh. The Emerald Tavern witch looks so different with her friends, a happiness that would have been impossible to imagine at the Tavern just the night before.

"The filthy bastards had their hands all over the girl! It's not like I couldn't do anything! I couldn't just sit there."

The witch next to her pulls her hood back, a sympathetic look on her face.

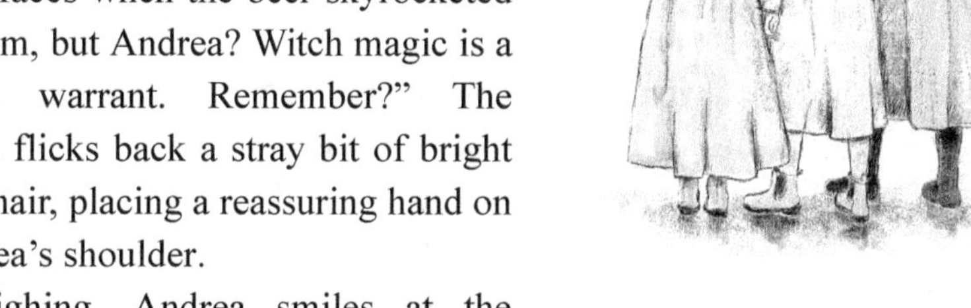

"I'm all for messing with the slimy creeps and I'd love to imagine their faces when the beer skyrocketed at them, but Andrea? Witch magic is a death warrant. Remember?" The witch flicks back a stray bit of bright blue hair, placing a reassuring hand on Andrea's shoulder.

Sighing, Andrea smiles at the witch.

"I know it was dangerous. Believe me, I do. But the look on her face Lilly. The barmaid wasn't even repulsed? Like this treatment was something she put up with a lot. Like those men were just something she had to get through to finish her shift? I can't even imagine what others had done to her, to make her so defeated. She would have barely been eighteen. I couldn't do it."

The third woman, who has been silent until now, lowers her hood and faces the other two.

"I get it. I do. I probably would have done the same thing. Andrea, you really should know better. You know how dangerous that could have been. We need you. Every Oz citizen who has been tortured and the many that have been killed need you. The legacy of the witches needs you. So please, my dear, next time..." The witch's solemn face breaks into a smirk. “When you do something stupid like that? Make it worthwhile. Turn their dicks to stone or something!”

Once more, the three of them erupt in laughter, never breaking stride in their walk down the Main Street. None of them notice the woman sitting in the doorway of a nearby Gilikin home, accompanied by a small girl. The girl sits, twirling her braids in her hand, watching the women pass.

“Why do you let the guards hurt us?”

The woman’s head shoots up and looks at the girl.

“I don’t have a choice, baby.”

The girl shifts so she is facing towards her mother.

“But we never have enough to eat! They aren’t helping us. They hurt you Mum.”

The woman cranes her neck, raising an eyebrow.

“What do you mean?”

The girl, sudden shyness overcoming her, looks down at her lap.

“I heard you in your room when they came to collect our taxes. You were making noises, and the guard was yelling, too.”

The woman’s face falls, a horrified look taking over. She sighs.

“Do you remember our neighbours?”

“The witches?”

“Yeah baby, the witches. They did something the guards didn’t like. The guards... they hurt them. Really badly. I won’t let that happen to you.”

“I don’t want you to get hurt either!”

The woman places an arm around the little girl’s shoulders.

“I won’t.”

Silence falls between the two.

“So long as I do what they want.”

For the last part of our introduction to the downfall of the great Oz, I bring you to the forest on the edge of the Emerald City. A farmer with a dodgy wheel on his cart.

The farmer pulls a large cart behind him, a grimace on his face and clothes dirtied from a day of trying to sell his products in the streets of Emerald City. Some leftovers roll around in the back. It was clearly a good day for selling. He sets a steady, albeit slow, pace away from the city.

The trees get thicker around him as he gets further into the forest. Dusk has fallen and glowing butterflies are becoming one of the few things providing visibility. As the cart travels the path, the ease of the journey grows difficult. The paths, the further from Emerald City, become more and more decrepit. Rocks and fallen branches become more frequent until the wheel of the cart catches one and rolls off into the woods.

"Oh, shit!"

The farmer unhooks himself from the cart and chases after the wheel. Through tree roots and rocks, across fallen branches and patches of grass, he follows the wheel, finally stopping at the base of an old and vine-ridden statue.

"Wha-?"

Slowly he picks up the wheel, trying to make out what the shape of the statue was from under the overgrowth. Stepping back, he trips over something sticking up from the ground he had not seen before in his hurry to the wheel.

He bends down and brushes dirt away, revealing a tarnished old plaque.

Dorothy of Kansas saved us all when she defeated our Queen, the Witch of the West. Now we thrive. Now all is fair for everyone. I lost my three-year-old son to the

WITCH'S REIGN, BUT WITHOUT DOROTHY SO MANY MORE PARENTS WOULD BE IN MY PLACE. THIS STATUE IS DEDICATED TO EVERYONE THAT WANTS TO SAVE LIVES. REMEMBER DOROTHY, BECAUSE SHE IS THE BEST OF US ALL.

After reading, he stands, sighing and stepping towards the statue. Reaching up, he pulls down a vine, revealing Dorothy's face.

"I don't know where you went, Dorothy, but we could all use a miracle."

CHAPTER TWO

Delia had lived in the other world her whole life. Not that she knew it as the 'other world' but more simply 'Earth.' She had grown up like most do, bumbling her way through school and eventually on to university. Her favourite place to sit and work was the desk near her bedroom window. Her favourite thing was her notebooks, even though they were filled with dull assignments.

"Why the hell do I have to write about how I actually feel? It's not like they'd know! Or maybe they would. Be a philosophy major, they said!"

Her throw was forceful, the paper hitting the wall on the other side of the room before falling onto a rubbish bin that was already full to the brim with her previous attempts.

"Okay! You wanna know what I'm really thinking? Fine. My name is Delia Woodbridge and I've lived in Under-glade my whole life. I'd do anything to get out of here... Anything."

Delia sighs, head thrown back on her spinning chair.

"I'm twenty-one and doing a philosophy degree because I don't know what I want in life. I don't have the money to leave. I don't know enough people to leave. I don't have a thrice removed uncle in New

York or an estranged aunt in upper Birmingham that can help establish me elsewhere."

Delia felt the tear down her cheek before registering she was crying.

"I've never been kissed. I've never been asked out. Hell! I don't even have friends. I read fan fiction in my spare time, like some delusional teenager that has to believe her favourite celebrity will fall madly in love with her. Somewhere deep down, as much as I try to deny it, I still dream of a guy with a foreign accent that accepts me, faults and all. So I just keep living."

She clicks her pen, then continues writing.

"So... It's just me. I'm, well? Nothing."

The night fell and Delia was still at her desk. Her attention was drifting to the photos on a pin board on the wall opposite to her desk. It was full of pictures, ranging from celebrities to family. An older woman appeared in many of them, sharing many of the same characteristics as Delia and clearly her mother. They are always happy, tickets and trinkets pinned by many souvenirs of time spent together. A black and white cat also appears in many others. Eddie Munson, Johnny Lawrence and Lexa are just a few fictional characters that also appear.

The cat broke Delia's attention from the pictures, jumping up onto the desk in front of her.

"Hey Mick. You caught me looking at your picture, didn't ya?"

Meow

"Do you think I can do it? Get out of here? I feel like I'm drowning Mick, drowning."

Delia spent a lot of her spare time, when not at her desk or sleeping through a lecture on campus at the local community park. It was a sizeable area, clearly beloved by the people of Under-glade. Mothers sat on a row of benches surrounding a large playground, children of all ages screaming and laughing as they clambered over the structure. A variety of retired citizens would scatter around the park daily, some taking leisurely strolls and many meeting to discuss the newest gossip with their friends. One older gentleman, Marty, would sit and feed birds, humming a song long since forgotten by popular culture.

Delia's favourite spot was behind the bench, three across and two down from Marty. Shaded by an acorn tree and away from the busiest parts of the park, it was perfect to sit and read or ponder university assignments. On this day, with headphones plugged in and a sketchbook in front of her, she was oblivious to all the park goers around her.

So she didn't notice as the sun went behind a wall of cloud.

Or as the wind grew.

Or when the clouds darkened.

She missed the parents, quickly scooping their kids up and hurrying from the park.

And Marty, hobbling away on his walking stick.

She didn't realise that suddenly she was the only one left in the park.

A shadow over her sketch was the first sign that something different was occurring. Looking up, she finally realised what had been happening in the park and the weather that just seemed to continue to deteriorate. Her headphones suddenly flew off, disconnecting from her phone that sat in her pocket and becoming a victim of the gale. She grabbed her bag, only for that to be wrenched from her hand as well. Quickly she lurched for the bench, wrapping her fingers around the sturdy metal. Her hands slipped down the bench, left hand being completely pulled away. Trying her hardest to grab back, she doesn't succeed, the wind somehow continuing to worsen. Her knuckles turned white as the bench became her only saving grace.

From the corner of Delia's eye, she could see the acorn tree.

Especially as it became uprooted.

Beginning to fly towards her.

The tree hit her in the torso, enough to not only wind her but completely knock her out.

CHAPTER THREE

Marcus Rightfoot, the wizard all feared, had a shit of a day.

The throne was digging into his back and he was ready to send the next guard to annoy him through a window if they came with one more problem. The captain of his guard, Michael Worthy, was next in line.

"Mr Worthy."

"Your Excellency."

"Please tell me you've come to announce the witches have raised the white flag and begged for death?"

A splattering of laughter echoed around the throne room.

"No, Your Excellency."

"Get on with it then."

Michael Worthy was clearly an anxious man. He wrung his hands together, shifting from side to side in front of the ruler.

"My liege. There has been movement picked up from the west. The

Coalition could not place an exact location but they believe it to be outer worldly."

That got Marcus's attention.

"Is there footage?"

Worthy nodded, snapping his fingers and watching a bubble appear in the air. The bubble cleared from opalescent to reveal a sharp picture. Noise emitted from the bubble.

Birds and forest noises were the easiest to identify, which soon zeroed down on someone's grumbling. The forest opening was littered with debris and mess. A figure was the only moving thing within the sea of destruction.

The figure spun as she stood out from under the tree.

"What sort of storm was that? No global warming, my ass."

Standing, her face came into view of the bubble, a streak of blood down her forehead.

"Where the fuck am I?"

Worthy snapped his fingers, finishing the bubble's transmission.

Marcus Rightfoot was out of his seat by the end of the transmission, looking considerably more irritated than he had before.

"Is it a witch?"

"No, sir."

"Which world?"

Worthy shifted in his spot, sweat beading down his face.

"Answer me."

Worthy stutters as he says, "She's from... Dorothy's world, my liege."

Rightfoot falls silent, deadly silent.

"Find her."

No guards moved, each too scared to do the wrong thing.

"NOW!"

CHAPTER FOUR

Delia knew one thing.

She had no idea where she was.

She slowly made her way through the debris, jumping over an overturned bus shelter, rock concert flyer still hanging on, trying to avoid the myriad of glass and crunching sofa cans under her feet.

"Stupid litter bugs," she mutters, trying to shake a plastic bag from her shoe.

While Delia wrestled with her shoe, a figure emerged from the trees. Once she rid herself of the unruly plastic, she turned, finally seeing the figure in the close distance.

"Who are you?"

"Your new best friend."

Delia crawled her way over fallen tree logs and way too many Starbucks cups towards the figure. As the figure came into view, Delia could make out her appearance. With her dark red hair, this woman used to be very beautiful. It was apparent, however, that time and life had taken that away from her. Despite this, her eyes were clearly kind, with a youthful mischief in them.

"I don't make friends that easily."

The woman snorted and mumbled something incomprehensible under her breath.

"Neither do I."

The two figures stood at an impasse. One staring at the other, each waiting for the next to make the first move.

"Where am I?"

"Winkie Country."

Delia cackled.

"Bullshit."

"No, my dear, not bullshit."

Again, the pair fell into a weirdly comfortable silence.

The woman moved forward once more, an eyebrow raised at the girl.

"You know you're in Oz?"

"Oz?"

"Oz."

"As in, *the* wonderful wizard of freaking Oz?"

The woman roared with laughter, causing Delia to sink further and further into complete and utter confusion.

"Wonderful is a massive stretch. You're not from around here, I take it?"

"Not from around here?" Delia spluttered.

"I'm from planet Earth. You know? The place where people know Oz is just a fairy tale?"

The woman shook her head. "Not a fairy tale unfortunately. Wish I could tell you differently. The monkeys aren't a myth, believe me! My sister used to breed them," the woman shuddered. "Nasty things they were."

"Tin men?"

"Tin man, singular. He was our first, I guess. Oz is good for firsts. Lots of weird shit happening!"

"Talking animals?"

The woman laughed again, more than amused by the girl's questions.

"Everywhere, most won't shut up. The monkeys had something going for them, I guess, no speech and all."

"Magic?"

The woman fell silent, a small smile decorating her face. Raising her left hand, a light spiral appeared from her palm and Delia's jaw went slack.

She dropped her hand as she took in Delia's paling face.

"Just for the record... I... I don't... don't..."

Delia fainted, hitting the ground at an alarming rate. The woman grimaced.

"I assume you were going to say I don't faint?"

The woman cackled once more.

"You're gonna be a handful, aren't you? I'm Ruby, by the way, in case you were wondering."

The woman raised her hand once more, a look of concentration spreading. Delia's body levitated, her head hanging limp. Turning in the direction she came, the woman threw a smirk over her shoulder.

"Sorry if you hit a couple of trees. Direction's not entirely my forte."

Delia's body followed quietly behind the woman in an eerie silence. The trees began slowly growing thicker, and the afternoon light soon disappeared. Every couple of minutes, Delia's hand or foot would hit some overgrowth.

"Sorry, love."

Eventually the tree line thinned again and soon Ruby and Delia were in another opening, this one containing a cottage.

It was an older cottage, walls crumbling in places and window edges fraying but clearly well looked after and loved. The garden out the front was an array of colour, roses and flowers of all kinds blooming into an almost blinding rainbow.

Ruby flicked her hand, Delia's limp form flew in front of her. Forward again they moved, the cottage now the clear destination.

Ruby admired the sleeping girl, certain that this was the person from her visions. The hair, the eyebrows, they all fit. A cat sat in the corner, purring softly. Nighttime crept in through the window, casting a shadow over the interior of the cottage. Eccentric decorations and colour were everywhere, the shadows transforming them from upbeat to uneasy. Ruby sat up in her chair as she noticed Delia beginning to rise.

"Wha-? Where? Oh, shit."

"I believe your words were, 'For the record, I don't... don't... don't, faint'?"

Meeting Ruby's eyes, Delia scrambled up from the bed she had been placed on.

"You."

"I won't hurt you, Delia."

Delia scoffs, staring the stranger down and pressing herself against the wall as if to make as much room between her and the woman as possible.

"Look, lady, I dunno what drugs you're on, because if I knew what they were, I certainly would have tried them already. Oz is a fictional place. Someone made it up, and you're trying to tell me it's real? And we're here? Dorothy was a little girl from Kansas that got murdered in the sixties. Oz was some kid's stupid made-up story about where she actually went."

Ruby picked at her nails. "I like your imagination."

"You like my imagination?" Delia choked out a laugh. "You really are something, lady."

Ruby abruptly stood up, making Delia flinch further into the wall.

"No idea what that story was, but I recognise Dorothy. You know her? We haven't seen her around this world for years now."

Delia could feel her nails piercing her palm, her hand squeezed so tightly she was begging to draw blood. The woman continued to look at her with an expectant smile.

"Dorothy is dead. Didn't you hear what I just said? She was a murder victim."

Ruby sighs. "Dorothy came to Oz after a tornado took her from her home in Kansas."

Delia scoffs. "I know the story."

Ruby raised a finger, silently pleading with the girl. "You don't know this one."

Delia seemed to relax slightly as Ruby continued.

"She was like you. Dressed weirdly and frowning at any piece of magic she came across. As Dorothy arrived, Oz was being ruled over by the wickedest of witches, Althea." Ruby laughs, pausing. "She was always power hungry, my sister."

"Your sister?"

Ruby smirked. "Long story and not the one I'm trying to tell."

Delia sat back, gesturing for the woman to continue.

"People knew her as the Witch of the West. Original, isn't it? Anyway, she was a bit of a bitch and no one liked her. Althea had gone 'off brand' of most witches. The majority simply wanted to be a part of Oz, but Althie? She wanted to rule them. Many people didn't eat. Many people didn't survive. I had a friend… she… um… died."

Delia leant forward, feeling a rush of empathy for this strange witch. "I'm so sorry."

Ruby waved her off. "It was a long time ago."

Ruby took a deep breath and continued. "Long story short, Delia? Dorothy saved us all. She elected her lion friend to lead Oz until she was of age, but when she was anointed, Oz thrived like nothing any Ozian had ever seen before. She was unbelievably loved. I don't know anyone that didn't like her."

"And then she disappeared?"

Nodding, Ruby stood up, grabbing a drink from the small sink behind her.

"About eight years ago, she was due to make an address to the Oz public about who would succeed her on the throne. She never showed up to the broadcast and the next day, the Wizard's Coalition announced Marcus Rightfoot would ascend to the throne."

Sitting back down, Ruby gestured to Delia.

"When Dorothy tried to defeat Althea, she came to me for advice. We stayed in touch over the years after she became ruler. A couple of weeks before she was supposed to make that announcement, she came to me. I play that conversation over and over in my head because she acted so weird," Ruby paused, looking at the ground.

"I still don't know why she acted that way, and believe me, I've been through every possibility. She asked me to look into her future and I assumed it was just because of pre-coronation jitters. When sitting down to do the spell, I instantly knew something was off because the pictures I was seeing weren't of Dorothy, but of someone else."

Whilst Ruby had been talking, Delia had let go of her iron grip, wincing at the pain shooting from her palms. "Who was it?"

For the first time, a flash of fear crossed Ruby's face.

"It was you, Delia. You in that field and then you... standing next to Dorothy… in royal robes."

Delia sprung up from her place on the bed, voice shaking as she addressed Ruby, "Well! Thanks for whatever this has been! I'd say let's do this again, but I'd be lying." Lunging towards the door, Delia inwardly cursed herself, as her hand couldn't quite grasp the handle. Once it had, she groaned; it was locked.

"I believe you are meant to find Dorothy."

Delia threw her head back, still clasping the door handle. "And now you're keeping me here."

Ruby stood to face her. "I don't want to hurt you, Delia and I won't. I also won't let you throw away our only chance to stop the wizards. Oz needs someone like you, Delia."

"Now, go to sleep. You've got a big road ahead of you."

CHAPTER FIVE

As soon as the snores began, Delia knew her captor was asleep. Slowly, so as not to tip off the witch, she threw the blanket off her, carefully stood and made her way back to the door. The silence was almost alarming, and Delia cringed as the handle squeaked in her palm.

Meow.

Delia whipped her head around to the cat that was sitting on a shelf straight across from the door.

"Shhhhh. Shut up."

Meoooowwww.

Delia's heart thumped in her chest. The damn cat was getting louder with each passing second. Looking over to Ruby, she sighed with relief, glad the witch seemed to have missed the noise.

Reaching her hand to her face, Delia mimed zipping her mouth shut. Turning back to the door, she once more went to grab the handle. She flinched as she felt something soft brush past her leg and, looking down, she silently cursed the cat who had decided to physically intimidate her.

"Shut up, you." She pointed a finger at the circling cat.

Meh. Meoowww.

"You prick."

Delia lunged at the cat, picking it up and wrapping a hand around its mouth. The cat let out a disgruntled screech.

"You be quiet, then I'll let you go when I'm far enough away, yeah?"

Mnph.

"Close enough."

Finally, Delia swung the door open and stepped out into the night, careful to maintain her grip on the cat's mouth. Through the garden and out into the clearing Delia got through, no problem. She reached the outer rim of trees and put the cat down. "Off you go, little bro."

The cat sat down and stared at her, as if starting its own little standoff.

"Shoo! Get!" She waved it away, the cat still not moving.

"You can go now! You're all good!"

Meow.

Approaching voices caused Delia to cut off the one-sided conversation. Seeing figures appearing on the other side of the opening, Delia grabbed the cat and moved them both behind a large oak tree.

The figures all wore different coloured shades of the same-styled cloaks, identical silver boots catching the glare of the moon. One of them, in a yellow coat, strode forward, clearly a leader of sorts. Flanked by men in orange and green coats, they made a colourful yet intimidating group. Reaching the cottage, the orange-coated one let out a gleeful laugh, one hand thrown out toward Ruby's garden.

It was instantaneous-the garden going up in flames. The yellow-coated one gestured and his two companions walked into the house. The flames from the garden lapped at the side of the cottage, eventually catching it on fire. Shadows loomed all over the forest opening, casting terrifying figures.

Meow.

Delia flinched, quickly placing a hand over the cat's mouth once more.

The two men that had entered the cottage re- emerged with an unconscious Ruby hanging supported between them. They brought Ruby in front of the man with the yellow coat.

"Ruby of the West! We got her, boys!"

The men let out a consecutive roar, the orange coated man sending another stream of flames into the already burning cottage. He stepped forward, Ruby's limp body held up by some invisible force. The green-coated man followed suit with Ruby's body now hanging in front of the three men. The man in the orange coat stepped forward, his body looming over Ruby.

"Not so scary, are we now? Can I?"

He threw a look over his shoulder at the yellow-coated man, and Delia gasps when she saw a small flame lick Ruby's cheek.

"No. Marcus will want to deal with her. Make a show of it, you know? Dorothy's favourite little witch friend dead on the Emerald Palace steps. God, I can hear his bloody speech now."

Nodding, the orange-coated man stepped back behind the one in the yellow coat. All three men raised their hands and Ruby's body hovered between them. As they walked back the way they came, Delia slid down to her knees, letting go of the cat. The cat walked around and sat facing her.

"Well, shit! They actually used magic, and they took her... What do we do now?"

Meowwww.

"Why am I talking to you?"

The cat let out a mocking reply.

"I guess we're stuck together."

CHAPTER SIX

The main street of Winkie Country wasn't too busy at this time in the morning; the time when the sun was only just peeking over the horizon. Delia held onto the cat as she made her way down the road, looking side to side for any form of danger and hoping that those men in the coats were long gone. Any Winkies that pass, move with the need of absolute urgency, only stopping slightly at the sight of Delia dressed in foreign clothes, and the cat.

Shifting the cat in her arms, Delia brought him up to her ear.

"You don't happen to know anyone here, do you? I could do with some food."

Meh.

"Helpful."

Unbeknownst to Delia, a figure weaved from doorway to doorway, keeping a close but distant space between them. The red hood stood out amongst the faded yellow exterior of the buildings. However, no one really paid it much attention.

"You need a name, little dude."

Delia held the cat up to her face, tilting her head. One unimpressed look from the cat had her quickly pulling the cat back to her torso.

"I'm thinking Munsie. I may not have Eddie Munson as my real life boyfriend, but I can dedicate you to him."

Meh.

"Don't sound too excited, little bro."

The unusual pair continued to walk down the street, the figure in the hood keeping up behind them.

"What am I even doing, Munsie? Find a missing Dorothy? Beat some scary ass wizards that look like they'd snap me in two?"

The hooded figure closed the gap, getting closer and closer to Delia before placing a hand on her shoulder. Quickly, the figure wrapped their free hand around Delia's mouth. The figure pulled Delia toward the nearest alleyway; Delia couldn't fight back, and the figure's palm muffled her screams. Turning Delia to face them, the figure held up the hand that was not on Delia's face in a silent plea for Delia to be quiet.

"I just want to talk. Okay? Promise not to scream?"

Eyes wide, Delia slowly nodded.

The figure brought the hand on Delia's mouth back down to their side.

"Delia, right?"

"And you are?"

The figure snorted and removed their hood, revealing a beautiful blonde woman with shining green eyes.

"Andrea Mikaelson."

Delia huffed, "Okay, Andrea. What the hell are you doing and how do you know my name?"

The blonde woman frowned. "I'll explain, just later… 'cause right now we need to move."

"Why the hell would I go with you anywhere?"

Andrea huffed. "You are in danger. You can take the chance that I'm not a murderer and come with me, or stay here and die anyway."

"Okay."

Andrea nodded and reached behind Delia, pressing an aged yellow brick. Suddenly, the wall began to warp and change before the image of an office lit by fairy lights appeared.

Delia snorted.

"What d'ya want me to do? Commend your interior decorating?"

Without blinking an eye, Andrea chuckled right back. "As much as I'd love the feedback, no. It's a portal, smart ass."

Andrea gave Delia a small shove.

Smirking, Delia stepped towards the portal. "We only just met! Smart ass is a little presumptuous of you. I like it."

Without looking back, Delia warped into the room. Any light from the alleyway was gone as Andrea followed through right after. Delia turned, looking around the room at the sparse decorations. Two beanbags sat in the corner with a small table between them, one lonely bookcase and a desk made the room.

"Sit, relax, put the cat down. What's its name anyway?" Andrea shucked her coat off and sat behind the desk.

Delia looked down at one beanbag and sat, letting Munsie climb out of her hands.

"Um… Munsie?"

Andrea snorted, grabbing a stress ball from her desk and throwing it from hand to hand. "Cute."

The pair fell into a brief silence, Delia passing the time watching Munsie investigate an empty tin can.

"I am a part of the Witch Resistance. We got word yesterday that the wizard sent guards to a rural part of West Country after an 'outer world' tip off."

Delia perked up. "Witch Resistance?"

Andrea sighs. "Long story short, the wizard doesn't like witches, the witches don't like the wizards and we are one of the few beings powerful enough to match wizardry magic."

Delia nodded slowly. "Okay, I get that. Now, I assume I was the 'outer world tip off'?"

"Smarter than you look, aren't you? Yes, the outer world tip off was because of your gracious arrival. Typically, outer world tip offs are small things that have somehow snuck through the fabric between worlds, like animals or a book someone left at their bus stop. It is typically never a human."

"Typically never a human? So you've had a human before me?"

"Dorothy of Kansas."

Delia groaned. "Don't tell me you're like that other crazy chick."

Andrea raised an eyebrow at the girl, stress ball that had been going from hand to hand, pausing. "Explain."

"Said she was the sister of the Witch of the West or something. Completely batty if you ask me. Kept insisting that I would be the one to find Dorothy."

Andrea leant back on her chair, stress ball resuming its passing from hand to hand, as a smile broke out on her face.

"She comes from a shit family, so I don't blame her for being a little batty, but Ruby is completely safe, despite perhaps being a little out of it."

Meowwww.

Delia cackled. "And that little guy used to belong to her, but some scary magic dudes came along and took his mother."

Standing, Andrea's voice faltered. "She was taken?"

Delia nodded, taken slightly aback by Andrea's sudden change in demeanour.

Forgetting that the other girl was in the room, Andrea began pacing back and forth, head in hands. Stopping, she turned to Delia.

"She's losing her mind. No one can find Dorothy."

Delia took in the crestfallen look on the woman's face. "Don't you have any kind of hope? There's no way?"

Andrea looked away from Delia to Munsie, who had now made a bed of the overturned tin can. Her voice whispers, "I lost my faith when I found out Marcus Rightfoot killed my sister."

Delia stared at Andrea, the stranger still refusing to meet her face. The silence lasted longer this time; Andrea's ragged breathing was the only thing audible in the room.

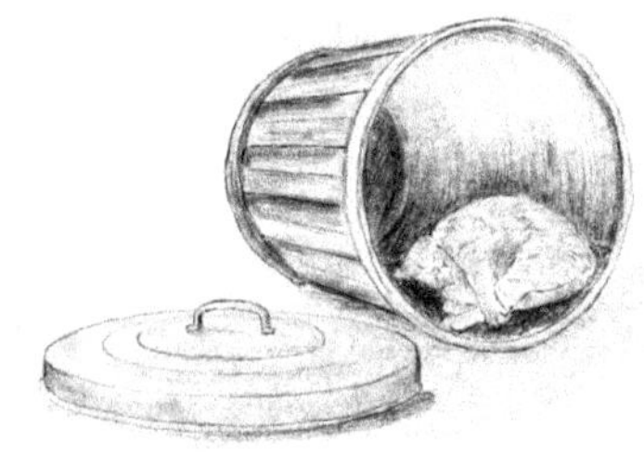

"You can stay here. It's underground and not the largest, but preferable to a public execution."

Delia stood, walking over to the woman.

“Are you insane? I’m going home! Not living in some witchy caves in a land I’m still not sure is just a hallucination from some really strong stuff!”

Andrea turned to face Delia. Delia could see the sadness in her eyes.

“It is impossible to voluntarily cross worlds. Dorothy is the only one that has done it in recent history more than once. I’m sorry, Delia, you’re stuck here.”

CHAPTER SEVEN

Let me bring you back to an earlier scene, my dear reader. The one where those three witches walked down a main street. Do you recognise one now? Andrea. The mysterious witch that Delia meets first. (She was certainly not going to count Ruby, who kidnapped her.)Now we jump back to Delia at the Witch Resistance. And Andrea, who really didn't know what to think of the mysterious being from another world.

Andrea sat next to the blue-haired Lilly and the older witch that had been her companions down Gilikin Main Street. Other women joined them, seated around the circular table, chatting to each other.

Delia sat to the left of Andrea, picking at her cuticles. She leant over and whispered in the blonde's ear. "Why am I here?"

Andrea looked over her shoulder at the girl, raising a finger to her lips.

Delia shot her a withering look.

The older witch broke through the mumbling in the room.

"Ruby of the West has been taken by the Wizard's Coalition."

Murmurs broke out around the room once more.

"Quiet."

It was not a loud declaration, nor was it a forceful one, but it carried the required authority. The older lady was clearly some form of leader.

She spoke up once more. “What some of you may or may not know is that Ruby truly believed there was someone that would arrive in Oz and bring Dorothy back to us. Many higher-level witches ridiculed her for this, claiming she had lost her grip on reality. It is my deepest and utmost belief that she was not wrong, that her visions showed her someone that would save us all.”

Frantic whispering broke out around the room, only a few addressing the older witch directly.

“How can you believe that?”

“We’ve exhausted every possibility, every angle, and someone else is meant to find Dorothy?”

This time it was Andrea who stood up. “Enough!” she roars, her voice echoing around the room, the dissent silenced.

The older woman nodded at Andrea, who sat back down.

"Early yesterday we received some second-hand news that the wizards had found an outer world tip off. A human outer world tip off, which you all know had only ever happened with Dorothy. The first person on the scene was Ruby, who met Delia over here."

The witch gestured to Delia, who smiled meekly as the witches turned their attention to her.

"Ruby confirmed Delia was the object of her visions, the one that she believed would find Dorothy."

Lilly scoffs, throwing her blue hair over her shoulder. "Oh yeah? Look at her! What the hell is she going to do that we haven't?"

Andrea tensed beside her. "Watch it, Lilly."

Turning to her friend, the blue-haired witch looked aghast.

"No, Andrea! I won't! We have had every magical creature in the country try their individual methods of hunting down Dorothy, none of which have worked. Then you sit here and tell me a human can do what none of us can?"

Opening her mouth to reply, the older witch silenced both Andrea and Lilly.

"May I remind you, Lilly, that Dorothy had no powers when she came to Oz? Most of you will not remember Althea, or how she was more commonly known as the 'Wicked Witch of the West', but I do. I also remember what her behaviour did to the reputation of witches everywhere. Dorothy not only defeated her, but restored the reputation of witches everywhere. What I'm trying to say is to give Delia a chance."

The room fell silent, eyes shifted back to Delia once more.

Andrea spoke up first.

"So, what do we do, Delia?"

Delia's eyes widened as she gestured wildly. "You're kidding, right? How the hell am I meant to know? I thought Oz was just a myth until two nights ago!"

The room broke out in arguments once more.

Lilly stood and pointed a finger at the older witch. "See! She's clueless!"

Lilly turned away from the leader to address Delia tersely. “Don’t you get it? Our lives are at stake. You take us down the wrong path on a whim? Which you will. We all die.”

The older witch stood, everyone growing still.

“All. Out.”

The witches began scrambling.

“Except you, Delia.”

Delia paused, sinking back into her chair. She watched as the witches left the room, Lilly throwing a scathing look over her shoulder, Andrea nodding in her direction.

Soon, the room was empty.

“I assume Andrea neglected to tell you my name.”

Delia met her sparkling blue eyes and nodded.

“Well, let me formally introduce myself, Delia Woodbridge, my name is Glinda.”

“As in ‘Glinda the Good Witch’?”

Glinda laughs.

“I can’t say I ever cared for that title, to be fully honest.”

Glinda reached over and grabbed Delia’s hand.

“I met Dorothy when she first arrived in Oz. Like you, she wore strange clothes, spoke strangely, and couldn’t understand any magic. She truly didn’t believe that she could survive Oz, but she did. And she thrived.”

Delia raised an eyebrow. “You’re telling me this why?”

“Dorothy was a fantastic leader because she went with her gut and I believe that’s exactly what she’d want you to do. Take your time to come up with a plan. Delia, we have resources and we have support so we can help you. Ignore Lilly, she’s sensitive...” Glinda paused. “Her girlfriend was killed about a month ago and it really did a number on her.”

Shaking her head, Glinda continues, “What I’m trying to say is that many people will do anything for Dorothy. We’ll set you up with a room. Take all the time you need.”

CHAPTER EIGHT

Delia sat in a blank room, one with no personal embellishments whatsoever. A desk and a bed are all that inhabit it beside her. A stack of books sit on top of the desks with titles from 'Oz Geography' to 'Ozian Musicals', from 'Wicked to Munchkin on the Roof'. Delia stares at the pile of books, lost in thought. She shakes her head and leans forward, grabbing the first from the pile, a book called 'Actually Me.'

"Written by Dorothy of Kansas? Of course she wrote a fucking autobiography. The cold case girl is actually the beloved leader of a fantasy land! Everything makes absolute sense!"

Delia laughs to herself, leaning back and flipping open the book to a random chapter. The chapter titled '*Kansas I miss you.*'

My favourite memory of growing up in Kansas was the fair that would visit every summer. It was full of things I never got to see from day to day. Full of something very close to magic. That was obviously before I knew magic actually existed, of course. The one spot I loved the most was always the candy stand. I'd sit under a tree nearby and think about anything that troubled me. Stuffing my face with this exotic candy was incredible. It was like some secret ingredient that solved all my problems. Ironically, the fair that travels Oz bears an uncanny resemblance and when I visited it in Munchkinland I found a stall that took me right back. I visit it sometimes now, to see if that problem solving prowess will somehow come back to me from my childhood. When things get difficult, I visit the Oz fair. There has always been something about a fair that seems to fix everything.

Delia closed the book and looked over at Munsie who was lying on the bed.

"Well! It's not like I've got any other ideas! Let's go to the fair Munsie."

Munsie meowed, closing his eyes and returning to sleep in protest.

The fair had unhealthy food, dangerous rides, and knick-knacks on every corner, just as a fair should. Except it didn't. The joy that characterises a good fair was nowhere to be found. People wore forced smiles and feigned enjoyment. It also wasn't as busy as the typical fair. The crowd crush? Non-existent. Only a few seemed to brave it.

Delia strolled slowly through the open fair, Munsie in her arms.

"This isn't the sorta thing I had in mind."

Meh.

Delia snorted, "Talkative, aren't we?"

Passing vendors that levitated their products and scammers that claimed they could cure world hunger, neither Delia nor Munsie could spot Dorothy's tree.

"Andrea gave us three hours, Munsie. Meow if you see sweets?"

Munsie was silent.

"Helpful."

Soon Delia became lost in the rhythm of the fair, the vendor's yells and the forced laughs creating an unsettling hum.

"Witch charms! Ward off their benevolent magic!"

"Official Emerald City clothing! Ready for a trip? We've got you covered with Wizard Coalition approved uniforms!"

"Books! Any books you could want! Learn about the history of Oz to things like how Mallory of the munchkins slept with her brother's husband!"

"Popping rocks! Chocolate pixie wands! Marshmallow, candy, anything your heart can desire!"

Delia's head whipped around as she registered what the vendor to her left was selling.

"Bingo."

She set Munsie down and walked over to the table. Meowing, Munsie followed behind her. Her eyes widened at the sweets available. From mints that promised side effects of levitation to fudge that claimed it could cure all acne, this table appeared to have something for everyone. Purchasing 'good luck ganache' and a slice of 'clever cake' with the money Andrea had given her, Delia turned away from the table and back to Munsie.

Meowww...

Munsie nudged her leg.

"Yeah! I'm coming, geez."

Munsie continues to nudge at her leg.

"What?"

Munsie walked off in the opposite direction, Delia throwing her hands up in defeat.

"Fine! I'm following a cat now."

Only after following Munsie did Delia spot where the feline was headed. A large oak tree stood just out of the fair action, a peaceful-looking spot. The tree cast a large cooling shadow over the grass. Just ahead of her, Munsie reached the tree and sat down, his meow sounding very much like 'I told you so.'

Delia pulled a face at the cat as she sat down. After unwrapping the 'clever cake', she turned to Munsie.

"Let us know if anything appears to you, yeah? I'm gonna eat this stuff, see if this cake is what I needed for those exams I failed last year."

Delia dug into the cake, frosting smeared across her cheek. She surveyed the fairground from her spot under the tree and saw as much as she had when she was walking through it. Leant back against the tree, she sighed.

"Oh, Andrea? I know you're following me."

Out of thin air, Andrea appeared.

"Touché, little outsider, touché."

Delia sat up and looked towards the woman. "What exactly am I looking for?"

Andrea snorted, "This was your idea, remember? I'm just here as your unwilling witchy sidekick."

Silence fell between the pair, both enraptured by the sounds and sights of the carnival.

Andrea sat down next to Delia, eyes not leaving the goings on around her. "Just look for things that stand out."

Delia huffed, eyes continuing to roam their surroundings. Eventually, her eyes settled on a couple of stand outs. First, one of the carnival rides was a colourful and rusty-looking spaceship called the 'FLYYER'. The second was a small country themed diner, a cowboy standing out the front handing out menus. The third was further away from the action, a small set of caves just viewable over the line of the fair.

"Those caves," says Delia, pointing. "What are they?"

"Literally just rock formations."

Delia poked her tongue out, explaining to Andrea the three places that struck a chord with her.

"What do they have to do with anything? I'm really trying here, Delia. I trust Glinda, so I'm trying to trust you and you're telling me you want to send people to a ride, a diner, and some caves?"

Delia narrowed her eyes.

"I didn't exactly sign up for this, did I? So take it or freaking leave it, that's all I've got."

Andrea sighs, turning to the girl, "Okay, Delia. But you're coming with me, yeah?"

Delia nodded, the pair standing.

"I'll send Lilly to the carnival ride and Sue to the diner."

The forest on the outside of the carnival was thick. Delia huffed every time her shirt got caught on a branch or she had to shake her hair in case of a spider attack. She tried to keep up with Andrea, but the witch seemed to be on a mission. Munsie followed close behind them both silently.

Delia called out to Andrea, "Thank you for this. I know I sound nuts."

Andrea stopped and turned back to Delia, a small smile on her face.

"It's all good. Glinda, she... Well? Let's just say I'd probably follow her anywhere and through anything."

Andrea clearly cared for Glinda.

Delia smiled.

Andrea turned back in the direction she had been walking and threw a comment over her shoulder. "And you're kinda alright without all the angsty bullshit."

CHAPTER NINE

Delia peered into the mouth of the first cave, squinting desperately to make out any kind of shape or interior.

"It's dark."

Andrea scoffs, a smirk creeping onto her face. "Well, I'm glad I said you were interesting and not smart." The witch clapped and a ball of light appeared in front of the two, lighting up the entrance. The light revealed little of the caves deep within Munchkin Mountain.

"It's not deep in."

Delia whipped to face Andrea, mouth open. "How the hell can you tell? I can't even see the end!"

Andrea began walking into the cave, the little ball of light bobbing alongside her. "Witch remember?"

Delia muttered under her breath, begrudgingly following behind. They walked for a while in silence before coming into a small opening. Someone had clearly lived there, with a pile of blankets in the corner and other items like a book and some old clothing.

Delia turned to Andrea, who was sifting through the blanket pile.

"Dorothy?"

Andrea stood and looked at Delia.

“Maybe. We’ll have to take some of this stuff back to the labs.”

The Witch Underground Labs were surprisingly high tech for an underground operation. Delia assumed it must have been the magic, some kind of mystical upgrade. Bathed in silver light from the multiple machines sitting around the wall of the room, Delia watched as three witches in lab coats stood around a pile of blankets Andrea and she had brought them. Andrea sat on a chair on the other side of the room, feet up on one bench, head hung back.

One witch turned to Andrea.

“I’m sorry, Andrea, It’s not Dorothy’s.”

Andrea looked up, face crestfallen.

The lab witch threw her gloves onto an empty table and walked over to Andrea.

“But, and I don’t know how to explain this, one blanket had a trace of dog hair. It reads as Toto’s.”

Andrea stood up, a smile growing. She wrapped her arms around the witch. “Lea! Thank you.”

Andrea stood back, a hand on Lea’s shoulder. “Were there any other traces? Of anyone else?”

Lea nodded, clearly a little frazzled by the sudden hug.

“The cowardly lion.”

Andrea laughs, despite their being no reason to, at least as far as Delia was aware. “That’s incredible!” She bounded over to Delia, who had been standing watching the pair.

Lea called after them, “Keep in mind these samples are old. They very well could have been from before Dorothy disappeared.” Delia’s face fell, Andrea still smiling. Andrea grabbed Delia’s hand, tugging her out into the hallway and giving Lea a small wave.

Walking Delia down the hallway slightly, Andrea stopped. “You realise how fantastic this is? Toto would never leave Dorothy's side; this has to mean something."

"That lab witch Lea, was it? She also said it could be old, like, nothing. I'm sorry, it was stupid of me to suggest going to those places."

Andrea sighs, pushing a piece of hair behind Delia's ear. "It wasn't. I can feel it. I know that sounds stupid, but trust me, please."

Delia stared into Andrea's eyes that were full of nothing but sincerity. "Okay."

The meeting room was packed. Even more witches than Delia's first meeting there. The chattering and laughing before the last meeting were absent this time, everyone unusually focused.

Glinda stood in front of the group, a solemn look on her face. "Most of you know we sent a reconnaissance mission to the Oz fair this morning. Three groups attended three different identified sites."

A witch three seats to Glinda's left nodded solemnly and Delia gathered that this was Sue, the one Andrea had sent to the diner.

"The first group, Sue and her apprentice, went to the diner called 'Down Country.' They found nothing of consequence."

Glinda paused, looking toward Sue and nodding.

Glinda continues, "The second group, Andrea and Delia, found traces of both Toto and the Cowardly Lion in the Munchkin Caves. Obviously, this is promising."

The room instantly broke out into questions.

"Why?"

"How?"

"How old are the samples?"

Glinda gestured for the room to quiet down, a couple of witches grumbling at the lack of answers. "Let me finish."

Andrea looked over at Delia, smiling.

"The third group, Lilly and her apprentice, were sent to the 'FLY-YER' carnival ride. A couple of passing officers of the wizard guard saw and engaged them. A brief battle followed. Halley, Lilly's apprentice, is missing. Lilly… Lilly is... well... Lilly is dead."

CHAPTER TEN

Delia's journey was never an easy one, but I'm sure you would agree this wasn't a great introduction to the land of Oz for the girl. Missing people, those killed in battle, and a public seemingly afraid to gather. Yes, Lilly hadn't been the most welcoming to Delia, but Delia still felt her loss hard. Lilly was clearly a beloved witch, for everywhere Delia went in the compound witches were in mourning. All the witches knew Delia had allowed the mission. Every look and every comment wore on Delia. After all, she'd never asked for any of this.

Delia sat in her room, which was looking slightly more lived in than it had before. A seashell shaped lamp cast a bronze light over Delia's figure sitting hunched on the bed. Holding her head in her hands, Delia continued to replay the events in her head.

Lilly scoffing at Delia.

Glinda repeating the girl is dead.

Ruby's body floating above that group of wizards.

Lilly is dead.

A knock broke through Delia's barrage of thoughts.

Andrea spoke through the door, "Delia? You in here? Wanna talk?"

Delia sighs, pulling the blanket from the bed over her head. Her voice came out muffled, "You're a witch, aren't you? You can open the door if you want to."

Andrea leant against the door.

"You're not a prisoner here, Delia. I will not force you to talk to me, nor am I going to use my powers to do so. I just want to talk, as friends?"

"Fine. I give you permission to witch yourself into the room."

Silence fell and Delia huffed, leaning back into the pillow, now a quilted lump on the bed.

"Are you okay?"

Andrea's voice was a lot closer this time, Delia assumed she was in the room. Delia shook her head.

Andrea chuckled. "How old are you, Delia?"

"Why?"

"Because in Oz it's only really typical of kids to hide under their blankets."

Delia laughs, "I think you've just been hanging around the wrong people."

Silence fell between the pair.

"I'm twenty-one, by the way."

Silence fell once more. It was a while before Andrea spoke up. "Talk to me, please."

Delia threw the blankets off and sat up, facing the girl.

"What do you want me to say, Andrea? I killed Lilly. Everyone here thinks it's my fault and Glinda still wants another plan from me!"

Andrea remained silent, staring into Delia's eyes.

"Someone is dead. And I'm meant to find Dorothy, who in my world died in the sixties and is apparently a great ruler that I'm destined to take over from! I hate to break it to you, Andrea. I'm not a witch. I don't have powers. Lilly did, and she died! What could I do against them?"

Andrea raised an eyebrow. "You done?"

Delia nodded, a guilty look on her face.

"There's an invention. It's quite ancient, but it is worth a look at."

Delia sat up.

"What is it?"

"A glove."

"A glove?"

"Yeah, Delia, a glove. It's meant to act as a conduit between people with dormant magical powers and whatever sort of magic they have within them. It essentially works as a test for people that don't have any obvious signs of magic. Any, and I mean any, fraction of magic would show up."

"How do we get it?" Delia breathes.

"We have one in the labs."

"It's not like anything else could get more screwed up!"

The sun shone, and the heat beat down on the witch and the girl who claimed she had no power. Summer in Oz was brutal, or so Andrea had told Delia, who swore that every summer as a kid she would end up as red as a tomato in the sun. The pair stood in a small clearing, Andrea hunched over the glove muttering incantations and leaving a curious Delia to get a good look at her surroundings.

The forest was mostly still, foliage swaying in the breeze ever so slightly. Suddenly, breaking through the stillness barrelled a small squirrel-like creature. Slowly, the squirrel levitated, Delia's mouth dropping open at the sight.

"Um, Andrea?"

Andrea looked up from the glove and smiles.

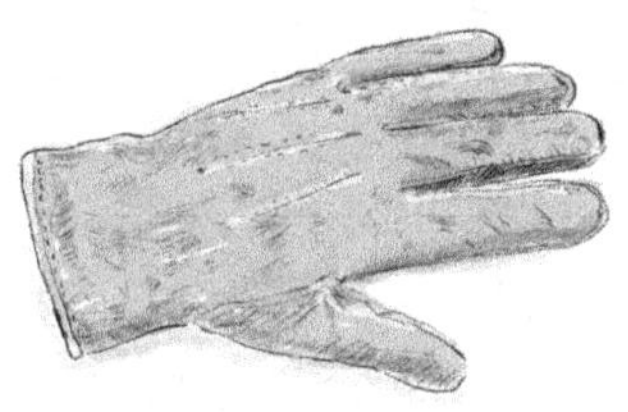

"That, my dear friend, is a curious little creature called the Matchika. They are weird little dudes, but some people keep them for pets."

Delia gaped. "What do they do?"

"Prone to bouts of paranoia and levitation they make for a hectic little balloon. Anyway! I'm done."

Andrea handed Delia the glove and stepped back.

It was an inconspicuous-looking thing, much like a gardening glove.

"This is it?"

Andrea raised an eyebrow, bemused by her disbelief.

"Yes, smart ass, put it on, yeah?"

Delia stuck her tongue out and slipped her hand into the glove. She looked up at Andrea for guidance.

"It will not hurt you. It's just a glove. Snap your fingers."

Delia snorted. "Jazz hands next?"

Andrea rolled her eyes, trying desperately to suppress a smile. "Just do it."

Taking a deep breath, Delia raised her hand and snapped her fingers. The glove glowed, startling her. With wide eyes, she looked at Andrea, who smiled.

"What the hell do I do now?"

"Whatever feels right."

Delia huffed, arms falling to her side. "You're kidding me, right?"

Andrea stepped back from the girl, her smile never fading.

Delia clenched her fist.

A tree on the other side of the clearing exploded.

Andrea whipped around, eyes wide. She ran over to Delia and grabbed her shoulders.

"That's incredible! You definitely have magic! You need it tested like, right now."

Andrea clapped her hands and steered Delia toward a portal that had popped up. Delia scoffed, thinking that she'd never get used to that. The clinical glare of the Witch lab came through the portal and bathed the pair in silver light. Delia looked at Andrea and smiled.

They stepped through the portal.

The laboratory was quiet at night, only one witch pottering away.

"Lea!" Andrea called, the witch in question looking up from her work, startled.

The older woman smiled and shuffled closer to where the two girls had appeared. "I assume you're here for further magic testing?"

Delia stepped forward. "How do you know?"

The woman smiled and lifted her hand to point at Delia. "The glove, my dear."

A blush decorated Delia's face. "I forgot about that."

Andrea rolled her eyes and grabbed Delia, pulling her closer to the older witch. Delia shot out her hand and Lea grabbed it, turning the palm over twice.

Lea raised an eyebrow at Andrea. "You realise this is going to take a while?"

Andrea stepped back and settled into the chair she had occupied that day after the Oz fair. She raised her hands, "Aaaaand... Go."

Lea shot Delia a sympathetic look and pulled her over to a weird-looking machine. This started a series of different tests where Lea poked, prodded, and frankly made Delia do some weird things.

"Hop on one foot."

"You are kidding?"

When they finished, Delia walked back into the lab and laughed. Andrea lay slumped in the chair, her mouth open and snoring loudly. Lea clicked to get Delia's attention and held up a finger to her lips. Silently, Delia nodded, and they both walked towards the sleeping witch. After reaching over to a nearby cabinet, Lea pulled out a large flashlight.

When Lea flicked the light on, Andrea jumped, and as Delia would later on swear, at least four metres in the air.

"AHHHH!"

Delia couldn't wipe the grin from her face. The apparently unflappable witch had startled so much that the chair had gone flying.

Andrea hmphed at Lea. "Great..."

Lea smiles meekly. "Sorry, couldn't resist."

Andrea sighs, trying her hardest to suppress a smile.

"Where's the chosen one?"

Lea pointed in Delia's direction and Andrea whipped around. She smiled softly. "Hi, Delia," she drawls.

"Hi, Andrea."

Andrea turned back to Lea. "I'm sure you want to dissect her, but are we done for the day?"

Lea shifted uncomfortably, like she wanted to disagree with her. "Can I speak to you?"

Andrea nodded. "Duh?"

Lea cleared her throat. "Alone?"

Andrea tried to decipher the look on her friend's face but to no success.

"Please?"

Nodding, Andrea turned back to Delia.

Delia snapped up from where she leant against a counter. "Like hell you are! Listen, lady, I…"

A portal appeared beneath Delia's feet, cutting her off. She groaned as she was dropped unceremoniously in the hallway outside the lab. She hit the door in frustration. "What the hell! Andrea! You piece of shit! Come fight me without magic!"

Pressing her ear to the wall, she tried desperately to hear what was going on inside, but came up with nothing. She groaned and slid down to the floor.

A new portal appeared suddenly, flinging Delia back to her room; she landed on her bed and unleashed a torrent of curses. Thoughts racing, and, with the incessant need to curse out Andrea, Delia grabbed Dorothy's book off the desk. She flopped back down onto the bed and skimmed to a random page.

I met James, or as you probably all know him, 'the Scarecrow' when I began walking towards the Emerald City. Little did I know he would become a beloved friend all these years later.

I don't get to see him much now, as he lives in the East on a farm. He has a beautiful family. His son is now ten! That fact alone boggles me. James wants him to spend his time on the farm, but

Nick writes me with dreams of coming to Emerald City. I always tell him not to hurry his life away. He's got plenty of time to decide. Mathias, or again as you all know him, 'the Cowardly Lion', sees James and his family all the time. They became quite the pair after our escapades. I always laugh when I receive Christmas cards. Mathias manages to somehow sneak into the shot of James's family and James always jumps in on Mathias's.

Two photos adorned the other side of the page, one assuredly the Lion family photo and the other assuredly the Scarecrow family photo. Delia smiled to herself. They clearly cared for each other and looked like they would do anything for family.

Delia closed the book and sat, lost in thought.

"Oh, Andrea?"

It felt like hours before Andrea came through a portal into the room.

"Yes, dear?"

Delia looked at the girl, anger clear in her eyes. "I will never get used to that."

Andrea backed away, raising her hands in surrender. "I come in peace."

Andrea moved over to where Delia sat. "You called?"

Delia sighs. “This is a long shot, and I mean a long shot, but have you interviewed the scarecrow? Does he still live on that farm?”

Andrea raised an eyebrow. “Yeah, they’ve interviewed him loads.”

Delia nodded. “Okay. He was best friends with the Cowardly Lion. As in the traces we found in the cave. What about him?”

“He disappeared shortly after Dorothy did.”

CHAPTER ELEVEN

Delia and Andrea made their way through a cornfield, the two figures cutting through the crops. The moon shone down on them, their only guiding point.

"Like I said, Delia, we'll follow the moon, and we should get there!"

Delia snorted. "Yeah! Sure! Like you said ten minutes ago! And in the meantime, I have corn husks in places I don't wanna acknowledge."

Andrea laughs. "Yep. Please don't acknowledge them to me."

The pair continues walking as Delia sent a sultry look Andrea's way, "Don't act like that wouldn't be the most thrill you've gotten recently."

Andrea snorted, muttering under her breath, "Unfortunately, probably true."

Before Delia could reply, they finally reached the edge of the corn, a farmhouse cottage coming into view. A light streamed out through the closed curtains of the cozy-looking home. A child laughed and a man could be heard singing, his voice reverberating around the field. Delia looked at Andrea and rushed forward, knocking on the door.

A woman, with straw for limbs and flowers threaded into dark auburn hair, opened the door. "Can I help you?"

Delia spoke up before Andrea could say anything. "My name is Delia Woodbridge, I'm here about Dorothy."

The woman's face dropped, and she moved to close the door, but Delia scrambled and stuck her foot in the way so she couldn't. The woman huffed, opening the door again.

"What about her? Hey? Don't you think my husband has been through enough? James has spoken to the authorities, and he doesn't know where she went. He's barely recovered now, all these years later. Who do you think you are? Coming to my home…"

Before Delia could cop anymore from the woman, Andrea stepped forward. "Glinda sent us."

The woman stopped, her anger dissipating. Turnng, she called into the home, "James!"

From inside the cottage came a series of shuffles before the door opened wider to reveal a male scarecrow. The woman shuffled away, and the man closed the door behind him. "Outside, we talk outside."

Without checking to see if they were followed, the man walked away from the light of the cottage towards a large tree with a tyre swing. Once he reached the tree, he turned to the women.

"I don't know what she wants from me! I've told her and helped her all I can!"

Delia stepped forward. "When was the last time you spoke to Mathias?"

The man's face fell. He shook his head.

Andrea rested a hand on his shoulder. "It's okay, James. You can talk to us."

He sighs. "We had a... well... argument, a couple of weeks before Dorothy disappeared. I always assumed we'd see each other at Dorothy's, well... her funeral. Obviously, we never had one, so we just didn't speak. It's been years now."

Andrea pushed. "Where was Mathias living?"

James opened his mouth, voice cracking as he paused. "He lived with his wife in the Emerald City. He obviously wouldn't be there anymore; it would have gotten dangerous for him pretty quickly after the wizards came. He could be, and I hate to imagine this, but he could very well be dead."

Delia looked over to Andrea, a silent begging in her eyes. "We have to try."

Andrea nodded, lost for words.

Behind Delia appeared one of Andrea's portals, and now recognising the familiar noise, Delia waved to James and turned, stepping into the portal. Before Andrea could move to follow her, James grabbed her wrist.

"You'll die."

Wordlessly, Andrea nodded. "If I have to die to find Dorothy, then so be it. That woman through there? She's supposed to save us all. To be honest? The more time I spend around her, the more I believe it may not be complete and utter bullshit."

James let go of her wrist. "Good luck."

Andrea nodded, stepping through the portal.

Delia leant against a tree, watching the early morning light rise. Her head snapped towards Andrea as she walked through the portal. "I thought we were going to the Emerald City?"

Andrea nodded. "We are. It's just too dangerous to portal too close. The wizards can pick it up and know where we are in a second. It's about a day or so on foot. We should reach it by dusk."

Delia groans and pulled herself off of the tree, cracking her knuckles and stretching out her neck.

"All-right then."

The pair began walking.

The sun shone brightly overhead, the midday heat scorching. The pair were silent, the environment around them having barely changed.

“I’m just gonna say it. How do scarecrow people reproduce?”

Andrea chortles. “That’s your first thought? Not, ‘how do they have scarecrow people in the first place’?”

“Well, it’s all hay, isn’t it? Don’t you need certain things?”

Andrea’s laughter rose. “You are something else, Delia Woodbridge.”

Delia smiles. “Well, if only all the boys felt that too!”

Andrea smiles back, falling silent.

“Boys?”

Delia felt the blush creep up her cheeks, “Well, I’m not exactly what they are lining up for back home. Girls too, I guess.”

Delia walked ahead, trying her hardest to avoid Andrea’s stare.

Andrea smiled, feeling the blush rise in her cheeks this time.

Just as Andrea had predicted, the large green gates had appeared as the sun settled. They continued onward, the brisk pace they had set all day never faltering. Eventually, they could see the crowd of people lining up to enter the city. Andrea reached out a hand to stop Delia.

“We are about to go through the South district gate. It’s one of the safer ones, but, Delia, this is still incredibly dangerous. Are you sure you want to do this?”

Delia nodded and grasped Andrea’s hand. “I trust you.”

Andrea smiles and squeezed her hand, “Let’s do this.”

People packed the party district. Socialites and guardsmen flirted, wizards leered at passing girls and any fear that was seen during the day disappeared into the drunken haze. Delia and Andrea walked through the crowds together, heads down. Yanking on Delia's hand, Andrea motioned down an alleyway. Moving in that direction, they reached a break in the crowd. The only person in the alleyway was a homeless woman whose attention seemed to be taken by something only she could see. They hurried past her and down to a doorway near the end of the passage.

Andrea let go of Delia's hand, stepping forward to knock on the door. The pair waited, the only noise coming from the revellers down the end of the alleyway and the muttering of the homeless woman.

"This better not be the freaking guards again! I already paid today's taxes!"

The door was yanked open and a scruffy older man stood in its place. His pants were a muted green, his shirt stained and frayed. He wore an apron around his torso. "Who the hell are you?" He peered, trying to make out who the figures were.

Andrea lifted her head and grinned.

"You piece of shit. Andrea Mikaelson, what are you doing here?" The man's growl quickly disappeared, replaced by a good-natured smile. He wrapped an arm around Andrea and pulled her into a close-knit hug.

"You got any spare rooms, Milo?"

Letting the girl go, Milo smiles once more. "For you, Andrea? Always."

The pair laughed and Milo walked away into the building. Andrea went to follow but not before checking back with Delia.

"Come on."

They followed behind Milo into the building and almost instantly hit an old staircase. The entire building was decorated as a cheap version of the city outside, with green trimmings and faded green pictures. Milo led them down the hallway at the bottom of the staircase, stopping at a silver door.

"All right, ladies, your room."

He swung open the door, and they both walked inside. Delia turned to speak with him, but the door shut before she could.

Delia whipped back to Andrea, who was now sitting on one of the twin beds. "Wanna explain what the hell this is and what the hell his problem was?"

Andrea smiles as she pulled off her coat. "That is Milo." Pulling it off all the way, she continues, "He's an old friend of the resistance."

Delia moved from the door to sit opposite Andrea on the other bed. "Okay?"

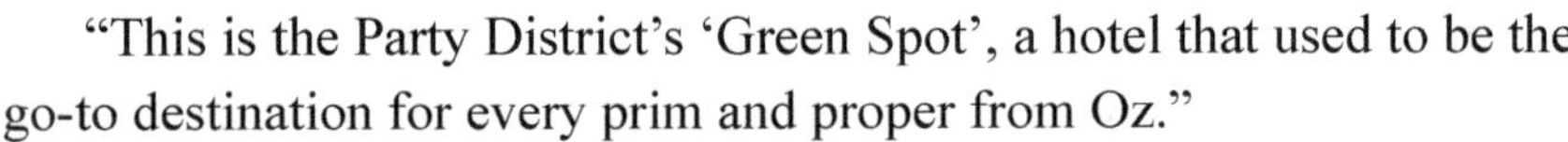

"This is the Party District's 'Green Spot', a hotel that used to be the go-to destination for every prim and proper from Oz."

Delia drummed her fingers along the edge of the bed, "This is all very interesting, Andrea, the history lesson, however, I didn't ask for."

Andrea rolled her eyes. "I'm getting there, love."

Delia threw her hands up in surrender. "Fine, go on."

"It's now what you'd call an 'underground spot.' The basement is a strip club and the second floor is rumoured to be a meeting spot for gangsters and what not. The first floor, which we are on, are the left-over rooms from when this did just used to be a hotel. Most of Oz doesn't know they are still here."

"And Milo?"

"Owns the place, his father was the original hotel owner. He means well."

Delia leant back on the bed, putting her feet up. "So we're safe here?"

Andrea nodded, copying the girl's actions. "Put it this way, if guards come knocking, it'll be for the partially naked people downstairs, not us."

"So, what do we do now?"

Andrea sighs. "It's too late to be walking through the city now. Anywhere outside of the party district has a curfew in place. We'd both get shot on sight. I also sort of have a warrant for my arrest in the majority of Emerald City."

Delia snorted. “Does that make you a criminal, my love? Here I was thinking you were an innocent little witch.”

Andrea stuck her tongue out. “Oh baby, you have no idea.”

Both girls moved towards the shared bag they had brought, Delia pulling out the copy of Actually Me and the glove. Andrea pulled out a book as well and flipped through its pages, speaking to Delia as she did so.

“Judging by the information provided by James, Mathias’s apartment is on the upper side. It is going to be difficult and stupidly dangerous, as the palace is just about a stone’s throw away.”

Delia hummed an acknowledgement, flipping through her book.

“It’s likely that the Coalition has planted bugs in the apartment. If Mathias had remained when Dorothy disappeared, they would have considered him a sympathiser and kept him under surveillance.

Delia looked over at Andrea, whose concentration was still on the book, despite the information she was providing.

“I will cast an appearance spell so I don’t look like myself. It will allow us to move quicker if I don’t have to stick to the shadows.”

Delia interrupts. “So you won’t be with me?”

Andrea looked up from the book, a soft smile on her face. “You’ll be fine. I won’t be far away, we’ll be able to see each other the whole time. One thing though…”

Delia groaned.

“Transformation spells are powerful, meaning I can’t use any other magic whilst transformed. We’ll be vulnerable, meaning that you either put the glove on and risk blowing someone up or be defenceless the entire time.”

“So, nothing to worry about, then?”

Andrea laughs. “Nope. Completely solid plan.”

CHAPTER TWELVE

It was still a little dark when the two figures slipped out of the door to the Green Spot, one muttering about how cold it was and one fiddling with the glove on her hand. A small bit of morning light gave the pair a bit more vision.

Andrea stood back up onto the step, finding a bit of warmth in the doorway. "No one can see you, remember? The alleyway is shrouded."

Down the end of the alleyway, the pair could see the occasional reveller pass through the main road, the early morning meaning only those that were too drunk to leave the night before were left.

Andrea flicked her hand and a rubbish bin flew from by the pair to the end of the alleyway, hitting the invisible force field at the end. She flicked her hand back, and the bin landed cleanly just in front of where Delia stood.

Delia looked at her and Andrea nodded. "Do it."

Breathing deeply, Delia flicked her gloved hand like Andrea had done before. Almost identically, the rubbish bin flew to the invisible shield.

Andrea flicked it back to Delia.

"Again."

Back and forth the pair went with the rubbish bin, falling into a wordless rhythm. Suddenly, the door flew open behind Andrea, knocking her on the shoulder.

"Owww."

"Sorry, love." Milo smiles.

He shimmied out from the door, Andrea shooting him a withering look.

"I'd get moving, ladies. It's six thirty and the guards usually arrive for daily tolls around seven."

"Well, Milo, it's always a pleasure!" Andrea jumped down from the step to stand next to Delia, grabbing her hand. Delia waved as Milo tipped an imaginary hat at the pair as they disappeared down the alleyway towards the Main Street. As they reached the precipice, Andrea stopped.

"Ready?"

Delia nodded, letting go of Andrea's hand.

Andrea whispered under her breath, and slowly her appearance shifted as well. Her blonde hair began to darken and lengthen, cascades of brunette locks falling around her shoulders. Her eyes glowed a bright cerulean. Andrea's clothes changed to a version of the Emerald City uniform.

Delia looked on, her mouth wide open.

As Andrea finished transforming, she looked at Delia. "What?"

"You... You… Are, huh?"

Andrea chuckles at the girl's expense. "English, dear."

"I thought you were being incognito?"

Andrea furrowed her eyebrows and gestured down to her outfit. "I am?"

"You… You're hot! How is that going to go unnoticed?"

Andrea gasps in a fake sense of shock. "What are you saying about my normal appearance?"

"I-well... Shut up."

Andrea chortles, laughter rising in her throat. "Let's just get on with this, yes? Give you a chance to collect your thoughts."

Without looking back, Andrea walked into Main Street, leaving a stuttering Delia to follow quickly behind her. They walked together through the Party District, neither of them finding any danger from the left over drunks and homeless. Eventually, up ahead, they could see the gate for Midtown. At this time, Midtown was buzzing with those on their way to work. A little before the gates, Andrea turned to Delia.

"You remember the plan, right? Stick to the buildings, keep your head down and if guards stop you? Don't, under any circumstances, speak to them."

Delia nodded, her heart feeling like it was beating in her throat. The pair separated as they reached the gates, blending into the rush of morning workers. Midtown was clearly a working district, with shops and factories on every corner. A spattering of rain made everything a little damp. Guards separated a path through the crowd, anyone in their way dodging desperately out of it. To avoid both the crowd and the rain, homeless people squeezed themselves into any available doorway or space for shelter. Everyone, homeless and workers alike, were skeletal, hunger clearly not discriminating. Three guards stood over a man, kicking and yelling, the man either dead or too injured to respond. A woman lies slumped against the bakery, lifeless.

Delia's eyes widened at the dead woman, her breath quickly increasing. She stopped, almost frozen at the sad and confronting sight. Eventually she seemed to shake it off and began moving again, but before she could get far, a hand shot out to stop her.

"What do we have here? This isn't Emerald City standard."

Delia felt her blood run cold.

Quickly, the person who grabbed her turned her to face them.

The guard pulled Delia closer by the front of her shirt, openly looking down at her chest as he did so.

"You're a pretty little thing, aren't you?" Delia gagged. The smell of alcohol on his breath was overwhelming.

"How about I forget this little wardrobe malfunction and you come with me? I bet you'd look better without clothes at all."

Delia tensed as the man groped her. "I'll make it good for you."

Suddenly, the guard went flying back into the brick wall, away from Delia. The crack was unmistakable as his head made contact, and he slumped down against the wall, close to the dead woman. Delia couldn't tell if he was alive.

Quickly, she whipped around and met Andrea's normal eyes through the crowd.

'Are you okay?' she mouthed.

Delia nodded.

"Andrea Mikaelson! Stop in the name of the Wizard."

Frantically, Andrea looked around as guards descended on her. She turned and spotted an alleyway, not looking back before sprinting away.

Delia watched as she fled. Now, alone.

Delia looked down at the small scrap of paper in her hand, peering desperately to make out the number Andrea had scribbled down.

Repeatedly, she looked up at the different buildings until settling on a large double story.

"Ninety-seven?"

She looked for a number before finding one hidden behind an overgrown plant.

"Hey. It's empty. Let's go." Delia flinched as Andrea suddenly stood next to her, she swore that she'd never get used to portalling.

"I..." Before Delia could continue, Andrea had opened the door to the apartment and began climbing the stairs. Delia scrambled after her.

The apartment was sparsely decorated and looked as if it had already been searched through. Separating, the pair went to investigate on opposite sides of the living space. Andrea began rifling through a filing cabinet, and Delia scanned the room.

Finding nothing, Delia sighed and threw her head back. Quickly, she whipped her head around to a bright light that had caught her eye. On the roof sat a small circle of bright green light that had moved.

"Um, Andrea?"

Before Delia could show her the discovery, a bang sounded from downstairs. Andrea whipped around, eyebrows wide. She pressed a finger to her mouth.

Hide!

Frantically, Delia looked around, settling on diving behind the couch as her cover. Andrea quickly pulled open a bare cupboard and stepped in, leaving the door open a small fraction. Voices echoed up the staircase as a group of people made their way into the apartment. A woman's authoritative voice rang out.

"Look around, you arrogant pricks. The sensors don't lie. Someone was, or is, still here."

Delia shook as she clung to the back of the couch. Quiet scratching noises echoed in her ear, so she leant back to investigate the couch. Letters had appeared, as if someone was writing.

DON'T MOVE.

Delia peered over the couch to the cupboard where Andrea stood. As they their eyes met, Andrea frowned and gestured frantically for Delia to hide back down. Delia did, but not before seeing the face of the woman.

Glinda.

It was freaking Glinda.

Delia felt her breath quicken, hands shaking. It would have been incredibly easy not to recognise her, but it had to be her. Her cheekbones and sparkling eyes were unmistakable. The eyeliner only enhancing her beautiful eyes. The scowl on her face made her almost unrecognisable, the kind old woman Delia had met at the Witch Underground gone.

Andrea could see everything from her spot in the cupboard, including the image of her beloved mentor, apparently working for the wizard. Her heart shattered, the pieces feeling unbelievably suffocating. She watched as a wizard slowly approached the couch where Delia hid.

Without missing a beat, Andrea jumped from the cupboard, causing everyone in the room to switch their attention to her.

Glinda sneers as she took in Andrea. "Of course it's you."

Andrea looked at Glinda, tears in her eyes. "I don't even know what to say, Glinda. I would have followed you through anything. This is unbelievable."

Glinda waved a hand. "Yeah? Well, you should have known better than to trust anyone. Shit happens, Andrea."

Without letting Andrea reply, Glinda motioned to the guards, who leapt forward to grab her. Andrea just slipped from their grip and began sprinting down the stairs. Spells began to be thrown, Andrea both expertly deflecting and attacking them. Throwing her arm up, Andrea got a spell through Glinda's defences, sending her flying across the room. Almost instantly, the guards stopped their attack on Andrea and the witch used this distraction to run out the door.

As Glinda sat up she saw the guards rushing to her side. "What are you doing? Go after her, you idiots!" she shouts.

Realising their mistake, the guards rushed for the door, leaving Glinda alone in the apartment. Glinda stood, wiping dust from her dress, and gave the space one last glance before sweeping down the stairs after them.

Delia stood up as soon as she was sure the apartment was clear. Her eyes locked to the spot Andrea had sent Glinda. She sighed and went back to the job neither of them had gotten very far through, searching the apartment. Walking over, she opened the cupboard Andrea had hidden in. Most of it was empty except for a few items at the bottom. She grazed her fingers around the wall of the cupboard before stopping at an unusual dip in the brick.

Delia pressed down; a small shelf popped out of the wall, revealing papers someone had hurriedly crammed into the compartment. She pulled them out and walked over to the couch she had hidden behind. "Okay, Mathias. Let's see what you've got in the dodgy spy movie compartment."

Pulling the biggest piece from the pile, Delia leant back and inspected it. It was a map of Oz, a large red circle in the west. Delia tapped the paper. "What was in the West? Ummmm..." She rubbed a tired hand across her face. "Ruby's cottage? Huh?"

Delia sat the paper next to her and picked up the next one on top of the pile. With scribbled letters and a dainty signature, it was clearly a letter.

My dear Ruby,

I know you worry about Dorothy. We all do. I'm sure it will not be long before she can return to us again. She may even be closer than we realise. Marcus Rightfoot has already turned this beautiful city into a living nightmare. It is my hope that within the next few days, I will have the opportunity to flee.

Please send for James and make sure his family is okay. I know the last thing he'd want is for me to turn up on his doorstep, newly wanted fugitive and all. This may very well be my last communication with you, so be careful and know that dark days are ahead of us.

Mathias.

Delia sighed and placed the letter on top of the map. "Glinda is working with the wizard. Mathias had some weird pen pal thing with the sister of the Wicked Witch of the West. Andrea is in trouble." Delia paused. "Why am I talking to myself? Where's Munsie when you need him?"

CHAPTER THIRTEEN

Delia clutched the third piece of paper to her chest as she surveyed the surrounding street. On the piece of paper was a poem.

On an emerald wave I go. Leaving my life behind. I follow my friend. I will forever. She runs from the danger, time slipping away. I will do my utmost to protect her until my dying day. So I head to the East or to the South or maybe in the middle where the earth meets the mouth. Goodbye dear friends, I hope to see you soon for now I travel, along with the moon.

"East and South I go. Then find the talking lion who will help me find Dorothy. Then Dorothy can help me back to my shithole of a life! Simple!"

Delia began walking. "Why am I still talking to myself?"

Delia stood where the earth meets the mouth, a rocky outlook on the barriers of East and South Country. The waves were intense, and the wind whipped her hair into a mess. Other than dark storm clouds, she could see nothing to do with Mathias or Dorothy.

The cold chilled her to the bone.

"You shouldn't have come here."

Delia turned, eyes widening at the man's unmistakable guard uniform. Trying desperately to calm her beating heart, she replies, "And why is that?"

"Because I've been looking for you, Delia Woodbridge."

"Who would you be?"

The man tipped his hat. "Captain of the Guard, Michael Worthy. I report to the great and powerful."

Delia's eyes widened, and she turned to run. Michael snapped his fingers and just as Ruby's body had done weeks ago, Delia went flying into the air, limp. She gasped for air; the wizard was restricting her air flow.

"I take it you were with the witch in Emerald City? Feel free to nod if I'm getting close." He slowly approached the girl and raised a hand to her cheek. "You were both in Mathias's apartment when Glinda found her, and not you?"

Delia tried to pull her face away from Michael's hand but his grip tightened.

"Wait! Don't tell me! She jumped out to distract Glinda…" Michael Worthy stopped, suddenly lost in thought. "You're not together, are you? Oh shit! You fancy each other. It's a shame she'll die soon." Michael's voice wandered off, his face peering over Delia's shoulder at the ocean. "Yeah. We found the poem years ago. No one knew what it meant, but we've had cameras planted here ever since. In case he showed up."

Michael pointed down to a rock that had a small version of the apartment's green camera on its side, the circle spinning. Delia silently cursed herself for missing it.

Michael turned and began walking back to where he had stood before, Delia unwillingly floating behind.

"You don't know how happy he'll be to see you, Delia. I might even finally get to see my family."

Michael continues to walk, the bravado in his voice lessening slightly. "Truly, Delia, I am sorry. I might be able to get you a minute with your witch. We'll see how generous he's feeling. As for Mathias? He disappeared shortly after Dorothy. You were chasing a dead end."

Michael snaps his fingers once more, causing Delia's body to fall again, unconscious.

Michael Worthy walked next to his horse, thoughts focused solely on the girl that floated behind him. The guilt felt like it was eating at his stomach. Anyone he took to the Wizard would die. He knew that. He also knew that Marcus Rightfoot was hell bent on this girl. Why, he did not know. He had to see his family one day. So, for now? He was stuck taking orders.

Distracted by his thoughts, Delia's unconscious figure hit a low-hanging branch which caused her to wake, shaking her head of any leftover sleepiness. As her eyes cleared, she locked onto the figure walking ahead. "Oi! Dickhead! Could at least give me a nicer ride for my kidnapping."

Michael turned slightly to smirk over his shoulder. "Don't make me knock you out again."

Delia huffed and muttered a string of curse words under her breath. She slowly tried to stretch her neck out, the invisible binds not allowing for much room. Suddenly her head jerked back, the view changing from the Oz forests to a dark space, bars blocking any details of the room. Andrea's voice rang in her head.

"Delia? Can you hear me? Are you okay? Please answer."

"How is this happening?"

A relieved laugh echoed around in Delia's head. "Thank God. You're okay. It's telepathic communication, I put images and sound in your head. This is my cell."

Delia felt her heart clench.

"Oh Andrea, I don't know what to say."

"Don't say anything, just listen. I'm so sorry. This is all my fault. The guards have been talking about it all morning. He caught you, didn't he? You don't deserve this, Delia, any of this. I- I'm so…"

Suddenly the image cut out and Delia was back in the forest, being led along by Michael Worthy, Andrea's voice gone.

"I'm so sorry, Andrea. If you can hear me? I'm coming."

Delia stared daggers into Michael Worthy's back. She clasped her stomach and began screaming.

Worthy whipped around to face her. Slowly, he walked over to her, an eyebrow raised. "What?"

"It's just…" Delia heaved. "I never signed up for this! I've had nothing against the wizard! I'm sure he's a great dude! It's just... she took me! I couldn't do anything. She's a witch!"

Michael sighed and snapped his fingers, breaking the invisible chain holding Delia up. Delia's body fell to the ground. "Look, I get it, okay? I never signed up to be Captain of the Guard, I was drafted."

Delia slowly raised her head, wiping away false tears.

"I haven't seen my family since the wizard took over. He believes that familial relationships are a distraction. My girl, she was twelve when I left. She'd be eighteen now. A complete adult that I missed growing up."

Using his distraction, Delia flies up, sending the metal binds on her hands directly into Michael's face.

The man falls back, knocked out and lying in mud.

"I'm genuinely sorry mate. I hope I can help you find your daughter. I just can't do that this way."

Michael opened his eyes, blood trickling down his forehead.

Delia ran.

The woods were dense, and Delia had no idea where she was. She kept running. She knew he wouldn't be far behind. Over fallen branches and masses of old tree roots, she sprinted.

Eventually, after what had felt like hours, she stopped, leaning against a tree.

"Surely that's far enough away."

The forest was silent.

Weirdly silent.

Like… No birds even.

No bugs, no ambient noise at all.

A light flashed, and a man appeared in the shadows of an overgrown tree.

He stepped towards Delia. “It’s you. Delia. From Dorothy’s world.”

“And who would you be?”

The man smiled and stepped forward into a little patch of light. He clicked his hands, and suddenly she saw the outlines of dozens of wizards surrounding her.

Delia only had eyes for the man in question.

“You’re...”

Marcus Rightfoot laughs.

“Yeah, honey. I’m the guy they all keep talking about.”

Marcus snaps his fingers.

Delia’s vision went black.

Andrea clung to the bars of her cell, hysterical.

“Tell me who it was! Please? Tell me!”

A guard watched on, eventually growing tired of her yelling. They stepped forward and hit Andrea’s hands, making her fall backward into her cell. Clearly weak, she pulled herself up against the wall, a palm bracing her.

“Delia? Please tell me that’s not you.”

Delia had stirred from her bed in the cell next to Andrea’s. She rubbed her head as if someone had hit her.

“Delia, please... Please don’t be here. I…”

“I’m sorry to disappoint but…” Andrea’s sobs cut Delia off.

“I’m so sorry, this, it’s all my fault! I should never have gotten you involved in all this. You’ll die because of me.”

Delia sat up quickly, any left-over weariness gone. “What?!”

Andrea sighs, trying her absolute best to swallow her hysteria. “These cells, they’re meant for people on execution. But someone will get us out. There are plans for these kinds of things. I know Glinda is evil but surely one of the other witches will find out. I’m not giving up yet, Delia! I… we, can do this.”

Delia stared vacantly ahead, memories of the interaction with the wizard flooding back, not acknowledging Andrea.

"Delia?"

"I met him. The wizard."

Andrea's eyes widened. "Oh Delia, I'm so sorry you had to do that alone."

"I couldn't picture it in the moment but Andrea?"

Andrea frowned. "Yes?"

"What's his actual name?"

"Marcus Rightfoot. Why do you ask?"

"He's my biological father."

CHAPTER FOURTEEN

Andrea and Delia sat in their cells in complete silence. A bored guard sat behind a desk, tossing a pair of keys around in his hands. Andrea picked at a stale looking piece of bread. Not much could be heard outside of their prison, so deep in the castle that no one would ever hear them scream.

A rumbling started, until finally, voices could be heard yelling.

"Can you hear that?" Delia strained her ears, trying to make out exactly what it was.

"Yeah, I can, it sounds like fighting?"

Delia's eyes shifted to the small window at the top of her cell. She moved over, leaning on top of the small bench to see if she could peer through the small gaps. The only thing she could see was a variety of lights, like outside her prison cell was not castle grounds, but a living kaleidoscope.

"There's lights? Colourful?"

Andrea perked up, "Flashing?"

Delia grimaced as a piercing light flashed by. "Yep."

Andrea smiles. "It's the witches. That's witch magic, Delia! They're here!"

"I thought the wizard guard was all powerful?"

"They are. It's just we have a chance now! We can use this as a distraction."

Delia slumped down from the window, collapsing onto the hard, dirty bedding supplied by the castle.

"I was told my dad left when I was ten."

"Delia…"

"I have no memory of him. None. All I've seen are pictures. The doctors called it a series of repressed memories. My so-called friends called it insanity."

Andrea sighs, wishing beyond anything that she could give the girl a hug.

"Repressed memories occur after trauma, but I never believed them. How could I be traumatised from such a nice-looking man? None of the photos were negative, no crying baby, no toddler having a tantrum."

"Delia, I'm so sorry."

Delia laughs, wiping the tear that had escaped. "I was so delusional. I wanted so badly to believe that there was someone out there that wanted to see me again someday. I completely ignored my mother's trauma because I wanted to believe in this man."

Delia fell silent.

Andrea waited to see if she would continue. "Delia?"

"You should have seen his face. It was so twisted, evil. His eyes, I don't know how to explain. He was meant to be the one that would drag me from my dreary life. And now? He's a wizard who has me on death row."

Delia's voice cracks.

"So, forgive me, Andrea, if I can't have hope. I'm still stuck trying to process that I'm not jumped up on acid and actually in a magical fairyland." Delia paused. "So please, leave me alone."

Unable to hold it back, Delia began openly sobbing.

Andrea clung to the bars of her cell. "You listen to me, Delia Woodbridge, I'm going to get you out of here. Trust me."

Nothing had changed in the two cells except for the lights growing larger and the fighting growing louder. The floors of the cells swirled in shadowed patterns of witch magic. Another guard had joined his comrade, this one chewing a piece of bubble gum, the other guard having never ceased his game of throwing the keys around.

A voice suddenly echoed throughout the castle.

"ALL GUARDS IN THE WEST WING. I REPEAT, ALL GUARDS IN THE WEST WING REPORT TO THE SIDE GATES."

The two guards shared a look before hopping quickly out of their seats. Blindly, the guard with the keys threw them onto the desk but overshot, the keys sliding off the desk and onto the floor.

Andrea's head shot up at the noise, eyes locking onto the keys.

"Please, Delia," Andrea began, "let me get us out of here. I know you don't believe it at the moment, but you are amazing. You're funny, you make stupid comments at the wrong time, and you have power!"

"Just stop."

Andrea groans, sick and tired of Delia's moping. "No! I won't. You wanna know what they told me in the lab? Actually? I don't give a shit if you want to know or not. Just listen."

Andrea paused for a moment, ready to yell if Delia interrupts her. After only hearing silence, she continues.

"Lea said she'd 'never seen anything like it'. You measured more powerful than Dorothy ever did! I know you don't believe me, but let's just work on getting out of here!"

Delia sighs, and Andrea strained to hear her reply. "Okay. Tell me what we're gonna do."

Andrea ran her hands through her hair. "I have a little bit of power. There is something blocking most of it, however, I should have enough to flick those keys over there to your cell." Andrea paused, and Delia's eyes locked onto where the keys had fallen in the guards' rush. "You pick them up, get yourself out, and then me. We run for the stairs."

"What do we do then?"

Andrea smiles, glad that at least Delia was invested enough to ask. "The witch resistance has had sieges like this planned for ages; there should be a group that was sent to free prisoners. We run until we find them. Then we make our way out as a group."

Silence fell for a moment.

"What makes you think their plan is going anywhere close to what was originally intended?"

"I have to have faith, Delia. This resistance has been my whole life. Witches in Oz are either dead or in the resistance. I have nowhere else to put myself. Nowhere else that I, well… nowhere else that I fit."

"How'd that go with Glinda then?"

This time the silence is harsh, the gap between the two now more evident than ever.

"That was cruel, Andrea, I'm sorry."

Andrea gulped, trying to find any words that wouldn't incite crying over her mentor's actual alliance. She couldn't, so she ignored the poorly timed jab.

"Let's just do it."

As soon as both of the women were out of their cells, Andrea pointed to the hidden stairs.

"There. Come on."

Up the stairs and through countless back hallways of the palace the girls went, running closer and closer towards the noise of fighting. Delia had fallen slightly behind, lapping at Andrea's heels so it was Andrea that first saw the two witches at the end of a hallway covered in rubble. One witch turned and Andrea could instantly recognise who it was Lea, the witch from the lab.

Almost instantly, Andrea took off sprinting and launched herself into Lea's arms.

"Thank god you're okay," Lea mumbles into Andrea's shoulder.

As the pair broke apart, Delia had caught up to the group, throwing a smile at the familiar witch.

"Hi."

"Hey."

"Delia, this is Hilary, everyone calls her Ace, and Hilary, I'm sure you've heard of the prodigal child."

Delia felt the blush attack her cheeks as she stepped forward to shake Ace's hand.

"I sure have." Ace grinned, a confident smile on her face.

Andrea stepped in. "This is all lovely and awkward and what not, but what's the plan, Lea?"

"They really need you at the front gates, Andrea. The combat witches aren't doing well, I'm afraid."

Andrea nodded and turned to Delia. "It seems we never get to work together for long. Stay safe, please."

Andrea seemed to hesitate, looking down at Delia.

Suddenly she stepped forward, pressing a kiss to Delia's unsuspecting lips.

Quickly, Andrea pulled away and headed toward the front gates.

Delia stared after her, mouth wide open in shock.

Watching the whole thing unfold, Lea placed a reassuring hand on Delia's shoulder, bringing her back to earth. "I'm going to need your help to get out of here, Delia. I know you have the glove."

Delia's eyes widened as she reached into the pocket of her coat, pulling out the glove.

Delia looked up, meeting the witch's eyes. "I've barely used it, Lea. To be honest? I still don't feel like I have magic. Andrea's the one that should help you. God! The first time I used it I blew up a tree!"

Lea frowned, saddened that this wonderful girl thought so little of herself.

"You are a powerful being, Delia Woodbridge. I have no doubt in my mind why Ruby of the West believed in you. And the way that Andrea looked at you? She's a hard person to crack, Delia, and for that? You must be truly amazing."

Delia pulled the glove on.

CHAPTER FIFTEEN

Delia and Lea walked side by side down each derelict hallway, Ace followed behind, eyes shifting from side to side, ready for attack. Jumping at a sudden noise, Ace instantly engaged a guard who had burst through into the hallway, lights flashing back and forth as they vigorously battled. Delia looked towards Lea expectantly, but the older witch just moved her along, leaving Ace on her own. From ahead came the unmistakable noise of fighting, making Lea stop in her tracks. The witch began jostling each doorknob she came across, hoping desperately that one would open. Eventually Lea tried a blue door which folded under her frantic attempts, opening into an unknown room.

Grabbing Delia by the hand, Lea pulled them both into the room without checking what was awaiting them.

Delia leant back against the closed door, hand to chest, trying desperately to slow her heart. She opened her eyes, only to slam them shut once more. Her heart felt as if it had gone down from one hundred and fifty beats per minute only to jump to three hundred.

In the middle of the room stood a lion.

The lion paid Lea no attention, eyes curiously roaming over Delia.

Delia felt her hands shake uncontrollably. She stepped away from the door and next to Lea, who stood examining the room. Momentarily, Delia flickered her eyes around the interior full of large green forest plants and a leopard print couch, but her gaze quickly made its way back to the lion as it walked closer to the pair.

"You're Mathias, aren't you? The cowardly lion?"

The lion laughed, a grin nothing short of human falling across his face. "I always hated that stupid nickname."

Delia stepped towards Mathias, very aware of the closing space between them, and how the lion seemed he could split her in two. "My name is Delia Woodbridge. I'm going to help you."

Mathias roars, thoroughly entertained. "Sure, sweetheart! Give it your best try!"

Delia put her hand out, willing Mathias to grab on.

The lion didn't move, grin still plastered on his face. Reaching out a paw that suddenly came to an abrupt stop, he smiled.

There was some kind of force field around him, one that rippled as he applied pressure. Like an almost invisible water wall.

"Got any tricks up your sleeve?"

Delia turned back to Lea, a panicked look on her face. Lea stood solemnly and nodded to Delia, both of them proceeding to raise a hand, Delia's gloved and Lea's not. They both closed their eyes, each hand shook.

Mathias stood, looking amused as nothing happened.

Delia twisted her hand.

The barrier shattered, magic exploding around the room, shooting through plant leaves and burning a hole in the couch. Mathias was quick to crouch down and avoid any magical residue. His eyes were so wide that his eyebrows seemed to disappear into the fur at the top of his head. Slowly, he stood up and walked over to Delia.

"Fine, colour me impressed."

The castle appeared to be in ruins and became more noticeable as the unusual group got closer and closer to the front gates. Wizards ran from all areas as witches pushed their way into the stronghold. It wasn't clear to Delia whether either side was winning or losing, but she would not stick around long enough to get a proper look in. The chaos was actually advantageous for the group, no one really noticing the large lion making his way from the palace with the two witches. Anyone who did, whether that be a witch or wizard, was easy enough for the two women to deflect, minds set on getting Mathias out. At the door to the castle Mathias stopped, Lea and Delia too caught up in fighting off a couple of rogue wizards to notice.

An all-powerful roar broke the battle sounds. Mathias lunged around to a wizard that stood just behind his back, hitting him square across the chest and sending him flying. The wizard hit the wall metres away.

Having drawn the two women's attention, they both stood in shook.

Mathias turned back to them, breathing deeply.

He caught Delia's eye and nodded.

The group moved forward.

CHAPTER SIXTEEN

The meeting room in the Witch Underground had never looked so depleted. Various witches sat slumped against the wall, all in different stages of pain and injury. Ace held her arm to her chest, trying to stop the torrent of blood from a large gash. Lea walked around, stopping at every witch before stopping at Ace and beginning to wrap a bandage around her wound.

There was only a small group of people around what was once the packed table. Most notable was Mathias, his large hulking figure dwarfing anyone in the room. Delia sat across from him, head rested in her hands. Andrea stood at the head of the table, leant against the wall. Her stare was vacant, eyes scanning the roof.

Lea huffed and dropped a blood-soaked bandage to the side. "Um, Andrea? We need more nurses."

Andrea didn't move, didn't respond, and didn't show any form of acknowledgement of the woman.

After a small portion of silence, Delia looked up from her hands, first to Andrea, and then to Lea, who was frowning.

"Just go, Lea," Delia muttered.

The older witch gave a grateful nod and scurried from the room. Andrea blinked, apparently attention now returning to her. "What the hell was that?"

Delia whipped around. "What?"

Andrea pulled herself from the spot on the wall and walked over to the table. "I'm in charge here, remember?"

Delia raised an eyebrow, incredulous. "You're kidding, right? All you were doing, Andrea, was staring at a wall. At least I gave her an answer."

The pair went back and forth, throwing insults like darts. The general noise of the room picked up as others took this as permission to speak.

Mathias shifted in his seat, eyebrows furrowed, then suddenly stood, his chair scraping on the ground. "ENOUGH!"

The room fell silent. Every single witch gaped at the lion.

"None of you are helping anyone by spending your time bickering! How do you expect to get anything done like that? Glinda is gone. We all have to suck it up and understand that."

The room erupted in argument once more.

Mathias was quiet, his next comment barely a whisper. "I know where Dorothy is."

You could have heard a pin drop.

The room was definitely silent for good now.

Delia was the first to reply. "You do?"

Mathias nodded. "Does anyone know what happened to Ruby of the West?"

"She was taken by a group of guards, I saw it."

"And her cat?"

Delia spluttered, "Munsie? What about him?"

Mathias raised an eyebrow, trying ever so desperately to suppress his laugh. "I'm not gonna even ask where that name came from. Before the Wizard's Coalition appeared and Dorothy went missing, she paid me a visit. It would have been about a week before she was due to make the heir announcement."

Mathias paused and took a long breath before he continues, "She had been having problems with her magic."

Andrea's head shot up, "That's impossible. She was one of the most powerful beings at the time."

Mathias shrugged, face full of sadness.

"That's exactly what I thought. Then she raised her eyebrows and transformed into a cat."

"The cat?"

"I believe so, yes."

Mathias inhaled deeply. "She then explained to me that her magic had been on the fritz. Likening it to a battery going flat. She'd apparently never felt like this before. Transformation spells were the only thing she could manage."

Andrea's eyes widened as she sat next to Delia.

Taking in Andrea's reaction, Delia turned back to Mathias. "I take it that's bad then?"

Mathias nodded. "They are one of the easier spells I'm told?" He looked to Andrea, who wordlessly agreed.

"Well, apparently the only thing she could really manage was her cat form."

Andrea hummed, a look of absolute disbelief on her face.

"Initially I laughed, thinking she was having me on. We had known each other for years, so I would not put it past her. Then suddenly she changed back to her cat form. I saw it in her eyes, the terror. I'd never seen her like that, not even when she was a young girl. The long-haired ginger cat may not have been my long-term friend, but as I looked into her blue eyes, I knew exactly who this was. The girl that all those years ago asked for my help."

"Munsie," Delia says under her breath.

Mathias crooked his head to the side, asking a silent question.

Andrea interrupts, "Munsie was Ruby's cat. Who tagged along with Delia here after Ruby was taken."

They all fell silent for a moment, thinking. Lea slipped back into the room, followed by a couple of witches that mustn't have been a part of the palace assault.

Andrea put a hand on Delia's shoulder. "Where is Munsie?"

"In my... my room."

Andrea gestured to a couple of witches that weren't too injured and they scurried from the room.

The room was deadly silent as they waited, no one daring to make a noise, much less any form of comment.

Sooner rather than later, the witches rushed back into the room, Munsie in tow. The cat meowed and thrashed in their arms, not happy with the apparent wake up call.

They sat him down and he shook himself, as if to rid himself of their touch. Looking up, his blue eyes landed on Delia, and he walked over to her, jumping up and sitting on an empty seat next to her.

Mathias was wide-eyed; he walked around the table and crouched down to the cat's line of vision.

"Dorothy?"

Meowwww.

Andrea stood.

"That's Dorothy?"

Mathias nodded, gulping for air. "That's her all right. We need to figure out how to change her back."

"I…" A witch stood, holding her side. She was clearly very injured and unstable on her feet. Without blinking, Lea was by her side, helping her approach the table. Lea sat her down, the witch giving her a grateful look before continuing. "I was in the underground team, getting into the palace by the tunnels."

Andrea tapped her foot. "The point please, Robin."

"There's a draining crystal under the castle."

The gasps that echoed around the room were almost exactly like something out of the cheesy old shows Delia cherished.

Andrea nodded, trying desperately to comprehend the new information. "You are sure?"

Robin nodded.

Andrea threw her head back, all pretence at the calm gone in an instant. "SHIT!"

Delia noted her distressed response and turned to Lea, who was slightly calmer but still holding a significantly concerned grimace. “What’s a draining crystal?” Delia asks.

Lea looked up. “It’s a structure made of crystal shards from a set of caves in West Country. It works to remove a witch's magic slowly, and after long exposure, a witch will eventually die. That would explain why Dorothy was trapped in cat form; she wouldn’t have had the magic to shift back.”

Delia hummed and begun pacing around the room. “Is there a way to reverse the damage?”

“Destroying the crystal releases magic it has collected, almost like opening a jar and letting the air fly out. Except Delia, none of us can risk it!”

Delia frowned, “Why?”

Andrea looked up. “Draining crystals slowly hack away at a witch’s power. They collect a lot of it. To metaphorically open that jar? It would kill any witch that tried.”

The room fell silent, each witch trying ever so desperately to think of a way to destroy the crystal.

Delia broke the silence. “I’m not a witch.”

CHAPTER SEVENTEEN

The room bustled with noise, each witch now enthusiastically throwing themselves into the new plan, the one that would involve Delia. Andrea's head reeled back and forth from right and wrong. She knew Delia wasn't a witch, but she just couldn't lose her. Not again.

She looked up from the table, glancing at her knuckles that had turned a concerning shade of white. Hunched over a map, Lea pointed to something, and Delia peered at it, nodding at what the older witch said.

Andrea's head drooped, her heart thumping in her ears. "No."

It was soft, but powerful. Every witch stopped what they were doing.

Delia turned from the map, eyebrows raised. "No, what?"

"I'm not sending you into that castle again."

Delia frowned and stepped closer to the witch. "What? Do you think I can't handle it or something? I tested as the most powerful outer world being that you have on record."

Andrea couldn't keep up the 'witch in charge façade', and let her face drop, sadness evident.

"You'll die."

Delia's face softened. "I'm not letting any witch sacrifice themselves when I could do the same job without dying."

Andrea shook her head, "You don't get it do you?" Delia's eyes widened as Andrea's voice grew louder. "The Wizard will kill you as soon as you step back into that city." Andrea's voice dropped back to her 'head witch' persona. "I won't lose you."

Standing directly in front of the witch, Delia shook her head. "It's not your choice."

Andrea's nostrils flared, she turned and headed for the door and magically slammed it behind her.

The room was silent.

"What are you doing? Get back to work!" Delia snaps before following Andrea out the door.

The hallways were the quietest Delia had ever heard them. Shadows made their homes on the wall, dancing a disturbing tale. She wandered for a little while until she caught the sound of sobbing. Stopped at an intersection between hallways, Delia silently cursed the maze of a place. Her eyes locked onto a figure hunched against the wall further down.

Delia walked slowly towards Andrea, her mind racing. She'd never seen the girl like this, so vulnerable. "Andrea?"

The crying stopped instantly as Andrea looked up.

"Please go away."

Delia shook her head and sat down next to Andrea. She kept her eyes set on the opposite wall, to not put too much pressure on her.

"I'll be okay, you know? I've got the glove and I think you've taught me a couple of things." Delia nudged Andrea playfully.

Andrea sniffled, letting out a small chuckle. "You're a pretty shit student, though."

Delia cackled, her amusement bouncing off the walls. "I wish I could say something like the 'teacher' wasn't so great either, but I'd be lying, Andrea. You're amazing."

The pair fell into a familiar silence, each just happy to sit with the other. Andrea's mind raced, replaying that comment repeatedly in her head. Hoping, clutching at any inclination that this meant Delia returned any form of romantic feelings. "I watched the wizard kill my sister."

Delia startled; her eyes wide as she turned to Andrea.

"It felt like my heart was getting torn out of my chest. Actually? No. It felt like my heart had shattered and the pieces were lodging themselves in every available organ. It was agony, Delia."

Delia was silent, at a loss for words.

"I saw her fall. Her body, limp. Every smile and laugh shared gone within a second. One word out of Marcus Rightfoot's mouth was all it took."

Andrea placed her hand on top of Delia's.

"I'm just going to say it…"

Delia's heart thumped in her chest as she looked into Andrea's aqua eyes.

"I like you, Delia. Like, really like you. I can't live with knowing he's taken someone else from me. Please, I can't." Andrea's voice wavered, her gaze on the pair's joined hands.

Delia squeezed her hand and let go of her grasp. She placed her hand softly under Andrea's chin, suddenly unsure of where her confidence had come from. "Can I kiss you?"

Andrea nodded, at a loss for words.

Delia leant in, closing her eyes as Andrea did the same. Their lips met and Andrea could have sworn fireworks went off in the distance. Andrea groaned as Delia pulled away. It was way too quick.

Delia smiled at the girl, a dumbfounded expression left on her face. She stood, hands reconnected. "Trust me. Please."

Delia dropped Andrea's hand and turned away quickly enough so that she didn't see her face fall. She began walking away.

"Delia, wait! Please..."

Delia felt the tear roll down her cheek before she acknowledged it.

She kept walking, not daring to turn back.

CHAPTER EIGHTEEN

The tunnels under Emerald City were dark. One witch had informed Delia that they hadn't been used since Dorothy. Munsie trotted behind her, enthralled with the magical ball of light Delia held in front of them.

"You didn't think of giving me any sign you were Dorothy?"

Meowwwww.

Delia snorted. "I would have settled for the simple, 'I'm not a dude, name me after someone else.'"

Munsie brushed past her and nodded in the direction forward.

Meowww.

"Yeah, yeah. Eyes on the prize and all that. If you are Dorothy? I'm not forgetting about this. We are having a nice old chat."

Before Delia could take another step, the tunnel lit up in an explosion of colour. Munsie screeched, the pair now surrounded by at least seven wizards, most noticeably Michael Worthy.

"You're coming with us."

Delia raised her hands, suddenly at a loss for any form of remark. Two wizards rushed forward to clasp them behind her back and Michael Worthy grabbed a very unimpressed cat.

Just like before, the tunnel was lit in a bright explosion.

Delia blinked, her vision adjusting to the bright and cavernous room.

The entryway? Delia thought, remembering vague flashes of the infrastructure from her previous visit to the castle.

In front of the little group stood a large set of ornate double doors. Their intricacies lent to its intimidating beauty, with small, almost tiny carvings of Ozians and famous landmarks. Michael Worthy gently pushed Delia towards the doors, the other wizards receiving the hint to move as their leader did. Worthy nodded to two separate wizards who stood by the doors and they moved to open them.

A great cavernous space opened before them. Wizards lined every inch of the wall, creating a walkway for the group. At the edge of the room stood a raised platform with a throne.

With one leg thrown over the side and his head resting back, the Wizard of Oz gave nothing but a bored impression. As the doors opened, his head snapped down and his face pulled into an eerie grin as he recognised whom his guard captain had captured.

As soon as the Wizard locked eyes with Delia, she felt her insides roar, like someone had set her aflame. In fact, she was so distracted by the appearance of the Wizard that it took her a considerable minute before she noticed the thrashing figure in a guard's arms next to him.

Andrea.

Tears streaming down her face.

And next to her?

Glinda.

Delia lurched forward, and the two wizards struggled to pull her back again.

"No! No... no, why?" Her voice broke.

The tears down Andrea's cheeks increased as she mouthed a quick, "I'm sorry."

Marcus Rightfoot stood up from his throne, eyes flitting between the pair, a bemused look on his face.

"Hello again Delia."

Delia's eyes instantly snap away from Andrea to the man who had addressed her.

He continues, "You'll never guess who I found entering the palace grounds earlier?"

Laughing, he gestured behind him to where Andrea stood.

"Apparently on a suicidal mission to destroy my draining crystal. And now seeing you here? I'm going to guess it was to save you from doing it yourself."

He smiles gleefully, "Wait! You two don't fancy each other, do you?"

Delia clenched down on her tongue, desperate not to say anything that would make it worse for the both of them. Marcus Rightfoot continued to glance between the two.

"I'm going to take the silence as a yes."

Marcus laughs. "Disgustingly sweet, isn't it? A stupid, stupid witch willing to die for her love, but it was all for nothing! Now I have both of you! I really don't like escaped prisoners, Delia. They grate on my nerves."

Delia began struggling against the hold of the two wizards.

Marcus raised his right hand and Andrea flew into the air, an invisible noose around her neck. Andrea thrashed, choking noises bubbling from her throat.

Delia screamed and lunged forward with all the might that she could, momentarily escaping the hold of the two guards. Taking notice of this, Marcus raised his free hand and sent Delia barreling back towards their hold.

Tears freely streaming, Delia screamed at Marcus. "Please! Don't! Take me instead! Don't hurt her!"

Marcus's smile snaps from amusement to something downright twisted within a second.

He clasped his right hand into a fist.

Delia watched as Andrea's neck snapped.

Saw everything as if it was in slow motion.

Her body falling to the ground.

Lifeless.

Delia was hysterical. "Let me go. Let me go now!"

Marcus sat back on his throne and nodded to the guards that held

Delia, both of whom instantly let go, allowing Delia to rush towards Andrea's body.

Delia cradled Andrea in her arms, sobs reverberating around the cavernous room.

Marcus leant over to Glinda and whispered in her ear.

"Take the girl, my love, and put her downstairs. Get Worthy to take the cat to the handmaids."

Glinda nodded and placed a chaste kiss on Marcus's cheek. He showed no response. She stood, straightening her dress, and nodded towards Michael Worthy who moved towards her. They spent a moment speaking back and forth before Worthy nodded and moved to the guard holding Munsie.

Delia watched through hooded eyes as Worthy left the throne room with Munsie in his hands.

Glinda turned to her and Delia tightened her grip on Andrea.

"I'm so sorry... this is my fault." Delia continues to cry.

Glinda raised her hand.

Delia flew into the air much like Andrea had done, however this time she flew forwards towards where Glinda stood. As Glinda turned towards the door, she magically floated behind her.

Delia stole one last look over her shoulder.

She shuddered at Andrea's lifeless body.

Then, she met Marcus's eye.

And he smiled.

CHAPTER NINETEEN

Delia floated in front of Glinda, eyes down. Glinda continued to keep her hand held at shoulder length, magically pushing Delia forward.

The image of Andrea's death played over and over in Delia's mind.

She shook her head, trying desperately to will away the memory, and took a deep breath.

"How can you let that happen? I know how much you meant to Andrea. Was all of that a lie? How could you keep up a ruse for so many years?"

Glinda stopped their movement; she was silent. Delia came to a halt.

"She was devastated when she saw you with them that day. You lied to her the whole time! You stood there as she... she... died!"

Delia gulped, hoping the break in her voice wasn't too noticeable. Her breathing grew more ragged.

"She looked at you like you hung the moon and stars in the sky. She would have done anything for you. You never saw the look on her face that day, but I did. It was heart-wrenching. She looked broken, Glinda."

"Stop."

It was meek, but it was powerful. Delia had clearly hit a nerve.

"She just died in front of you and you have nothing else to say? You're a coward, Glinda."

Glinda's scream broke through her sentence. "STOP NOW!"

Delia suddenly fell to the ground, all magical binds removed. She crawled around and spotted the powerful witch, body heaving in grief-filled sobs, hands clutching at the ground like it was the only thing keeping her alive.

Slowly Delia reached out to place a hand on the woman's shoulder.

Glinda stilled, stifling her sobs.

"Help me. Help me do what she wanted to do, what you claimed you wanted to do. Help me put an end to that monster."

Glinda's reply was almost imperceptible, but Delia heard every word. "I love him."

Delia's eyes widened, unsure of how to respond. Glinda continues, "But I also love… loved Andrea. He told me... he told me he wouldn't hurt her. He told me he loved me back. Lilly, poor Lilly, he told me he'd leave them both alone. He told me that her death was an accident."

Delia began rubbing small circles on Glinda's upper back, hoping she'd pull it together enough to form a plan. After a while of continued sobbing, Delia knew she had to say something, anything, to push her over the edge and onto her own side.

"Andrea is dead. Marcus Rightfoot killed her. We both saw it. He lied to you, Glinda."

Glinda wiped her tears on the sleeve of her dress and slowly rose from the ground. She looked at the younger girl. "What do we do?"

In the most condensed form possible, Delia filled Glinda in on the various happenings and goings, but most importantly, the true identity of Munsie.

Glinda snorted, a genuine smile spreading across her face. "Of course, it was the freaking cat."

Delia smiles softly. "Will you help me?"

Glinda nodded and pulled Delia down the hallway.

The crystal structure was even taller than Delia had first imagined. It was beautiful, like someone had stuck together shards of the rarest diamonds in every colour of the rainbow. She reached out to touch it and immediately regretted it, her hand coming away coated in some kind of slime. Glinda stood on the opposite side of the crystal, tapping her foot. Delia thought she looked more like she was waiting for a business meeting to start rather than waiting to defeat a powerful wizard.

Delia stood and looked around, but there wasn't much to see bar the draining crystal. Glinda had assured Delia help would meet them there.

Delia stilled as she heard noises coming down one tunnel that led to the crystal's intersection. She tensed as she noticed who the figure was that slipped into the opening. She was ready to raise her gloved hand and let all hell break loose until Glinda stepped in front of her.

"He's okay, Delia. He's on our side."

Then Delia noticed what, or should she say who, Michael Worthy held in his arms. Munsie's eyes widened comically when they met Delia's. He slipped out of Worthy's arms and made his way over to the girl.

Meowwww.

Delia smiled. "Missed you too, little man or woman, supposedly."

Delia looked from the cat and up to Glinda.

Glinda nodded. "You ready?"

Delia silently agreed as Glinda turned on her heel to leave down the tunnel, Michael Worthy taking her place.

Delia could feel her heart in her throat. She adjusted the glove on her hand, preparing for the next step. Before she could get any further, Michael Worthy cleared his throat.

"Delia?"

Delia looked up, eyes burning into Micheal's.

"For the record, I am really sorry, Delia. For everything. I know it doesn't excuse my actions, but I was doing this for my family. Marcus, he... took them. I don't know where they are or how they are. He promised their safety for good behaviour."

Delia nodded, concentration mainly on the crystal and not the anger that she still felt. "I understand."

Worthy's eyes turned to Delia's raised hand as it twisted, and the crystal shook. Soon the whole cavernous opening followed suit; Michael Worthy was almost certain the floor would collapse at any moment. Blindly, he reached behind him until he braced himself against the safety of the wall.

The trembling continued to grow and Delia's hair framed her face, held up by an invisible magical force.

Then it stopped.

No warning, just stopped.

Delia's head fell back, her eyes changing to a pearl white colour.

Time seemed to go still.

The draining crystal exploded.

Shards of coloured light flew all around the space, a kaleidoscope of colours.

A fine dust settled where the structure once stood, sand of dull silver.

The explosion hurled Delia and Michael Worthy backward, leaving them both crumpled messes against the tunnel walls.

Silence fell once more.

As soon as Delia could manage it, she was up and searching for Munsie.

Meowww.

Delia instantly snapped her head towards the noise, to see Munsie struggling to stand against the wall across from her.

A laugh echoed around the chamber.

"That's so sweet. Little Delia believing she could destroy a draining crystal properly. It takes warlocks and wizards years of training to make and destroy crystals. They're tricky pieces of magic."

Marcus Rightfoot turned to where Munsie had finally managed to stand.

"And you! I can't believe you got stuck as a cat... That made my day!"

Tears filled the corners of his eyes. "The great Dorothy! Reduced to this." He leant down and patted the top of the cat's head.

Delia knew she had to say something, anything, to get him away from the cat.

"Tahlia Woodbridge."

Marcus's head whipped around, and his eyes widened. Enraged, he strode over to where Delia stood and grabbed her neck, holding her up against the wall. "How do you know that name?"

Delia struggled, her feet kicking around underneath her, trying to find any escape, but the wizard was strong. "She's my mother."

Marcus's eyes widened even further, his hold on Delia loosened, and she fell to the ground.

Marcus spluttered, "I, she didn't, couldn't... is she okay?"

Delia gaped.

"What! Is she okay?" Delia's voice grew louder. "Why do you even care?"

Marcus stared down at her, silent.

"You left her with a small child because you had to become a nazi ruler of the magical land of Oz! You... well? You left me."

"Have you had your magic tested?"

Delia stared up at the man like he had suddenly developed three heads. "What?"

"HAVE you had your magic tested?"

Delia stayed silent.

Marcus raised his right hand, which sent Delia up and flying into the opposite wall. "Don't make me repeat myself."

Delia stared down at the man defiantly. "Yes."

Marcus ran over to where she hung from his invisible binds. "The results were what, exactly?"

An invisible force clamped itself around Delia's neck. She thrashed as it tightened slower and slower.

"I don't know, okay? They just said I was more powerful than Dorothy! That's all I know!"

The constriction on Delia's throat lifted, and she gasped for air.

"It's you. You're the one they spoke of. The sorceress to rule them all. Join me."

Delia spluttered with laughter. "You're kidding, right?"

A new voice replies, "Unfortunately, Delia, he's not."

Marcus whipped his head around, anger building in his features. "You."

Dorothy smiles. "Hi, Dad."

The two stared each other down, each almost daring the other to speak first.

Delia broke the silence. "What the fuck?"

Dorothy broke out of her staring contest with Marcus to move around him and address Delia. "I'm gonna deal with him. I need you to go find the witches; they're in one of the tunnels towards the exit. I'll meet you there."

Delia was amazed. This was the voice of the renowned leader she'd heard so much about. Managing a nod, Delia scrambled to her feet and hurried to one of the tunnels leading away from the cavern. From behind her, a light glowed, brighter and brighter.

"Hurry up, Delia!" echoed from behind her and soon her feet had taken off running.

CHAPTER TWENTY

Delia willed her feet to move as fast as they could, not stopping until she heard muted whispering. She quickly turned a corner and was face to face with another large cavern in the tunnels, except this one was full of witches. Lea noticed her straight away and waved.

Suddenly the witches stopped their individual conversations, mouths began dropping and gasps rung out periodically around the space. Heart still racing from her run in with the wizard, Delia flicked her head back around, expecting an attack.

Dorothy stood there.

Smiling.

Not a hair out of place.

"I know you all want answers, and that is something I intend to provide."

Delia moved to Dorothy's side, trying to get out of the gaze of all of those witches.

"However, now it is of the utmost importance that I speak with Delia before Marcus Rightfoot breaks through my temporary hold."

It was only at the mention of Delia's name that a few witches flicked their eyes to her, however they almost instantly return their rapt attention to Dorothy.

"I think you all know that now is the time Marcus Rightfoot is stopped. I need to speak to Delia and I need time to do so. I'm hoping you all can help."

Lea nodded and gestured for the witches to follow her. They all streamed quickly from the space. The cavern felt a lot larger, with just Delia and Dorothy. Delia could have sworn Dorothy's eyes drilled a hole into her soul.

"So…"

"We're sisters?" Delia interrupts, voice shaky.

Dorothy nodded. "Half-sisters technically."

Delia sighs.

"What's going on, Dorothy?"

Dorothy nodded, understanding Delia's despair. "Our father has always been someone that desires insurmountable power. Many years ago, he went to a seer that predicted he only had one way to gain that kind of power."

Delia crooked her head. "And that was how?"

"The seer said that there was a woman, one in another world, that would bear a child, this child being the most powerful sorceress or sorcerer ever seen."

"Hmph... Me?" Delia spluttered.

Dorothy nodded. "Yep, you. The catch with this being that magical transferral spells need a blood connection, one that comes from relation."

"So, he procreated until he received the all-powerful child?"

Dorothy laughs, astounded Delia managed any kind of sarcasm at a time like this. "Pretty much. Woo other world women, knock them up then test their children." Dorothy paused. "The worst thing?"

Delia frowned. "It gets worse?"

Dorothy smiles. "Unfortunately, yes." The smile left her face. "Magical transferral spells require the original host of the magic to be uninhabited."

"Meaning?"

"He planned to kill his own child."

Delia stepped back, spluttering out a reply. "You mean, um... he... planned to kill me?"

The mouth of the cave let in fighting noises, witches yelling for backup and a battle well and truly in progress.

Dorothy grabbed Delia's shoulders. "There's a cryogenic chamber off a passageway near the throne room. It will hold him. You are the only one that can put him there, Delia, the only one with enough strength. The witches will get you there. You just need to do the rest."

Delia nodded.

Dorothy seemed to hesitate before stepping away from the girl.

"I believe in you, Delia."

CHAPTER TWENTY-ONE

The Emerald City Palace was a battleground. An arena of death and destruction, wizards and witches playing the role of gladiators. Delia walked straight through the foray, head held high and occasionally flicking her hand so that any loose object or person flew in the opposite direction of her path.

Behind her stalked Marcus Rightfoot.

A furious Marcus Rightfoot.

With all pretence of the calm and calculated dictator gone, he moved like an animal on the hunt; blood pouring from a gash on his head seemingly not having bothered him at all.

He threw up a hand towards Delia, summoning a torrent of fire, then pushed it in her direction.

Without looking back, Delia threw up her right hand, the fire hitting an invisible barrier and being pushed up towards the roof, dissipating before it could catch on the building.

Only then did Delia turn, sending a smirk towards the frustrated wizard.

All background noise seemed to fade away as the two faced each other. Father and daughter on two very different sides.

"So, do I call you Dad? Or?"

Marcus laughs. "Please don't."

Delia smiles. "Dad it is then."

Before Marcus could offer a retort, Delia had begun once again making her way through the fighting. Only one thing on her mind.

Without looking back, she threw out her right hand, sending Marcus back several feet. Marcus's eyes narrowed back to playing the hunter and his prey.

The pair threw powerful spell after powerful spell at each other. If anyone were to watch their fight, they would see that they both seemed equally matched, one attacking and the other deflecting.

Soon the two found themselves at a dead end, Delia with her back to the wall and Marcus trying ever so desperately to cage her further and further into no escape.

The crease between Delia's eyebrows gave away her growing exhaustion as her defences became slower. Meanwhile, Marcus's attacks only increased.

It felt like the world stopped for a moment when Delia missed a deflection.

She felt like she could almost make out every detail of the palace's painted roofs.

Once Delia hit the wall, everything returned to normal, noise and action flooding back into her system. The image of Marcus, her father, stalking toward her.

"You done now?" Marcus reached down and wrapped a hand around her throat, pulling her up from the ground, not with magic this time but with his own unusually forceful strength.

Delia gagged.

A voice rang out. Dorothy's.

"No, she's not."

Dorothy stood behind the pair, surrounded by a group of witches, and behind them stood the unmistakable colours of the citizens of Oz. From the Winkies to the Quadlings, from early adulthood to late, all sporting the same serious faces.

Marcus's head whipped around to meet the steely eyes of his eldest daughter. "Oh yeah?"

His grip around Delia's throat tightened.

Dorothy met Delia's bulging eyes and nodded ever so slightly.

Delia knew exactly what it meant. Using Marcus's distraction, she kicked him with all her strength in the torso, and in his shock, she dropped to the ground, scrambling away before he could grab her again.

Before Marcus could turn after her, Dorothy and the witches had moved forward, sending a barrage of spells towards the wizard. The group of Ozians entered the fray behind them, the sheer number of people allowing for a considerable surge against the wizards. They all moved with handmade weapons, pots and pans and the occasional bat, no one afraid to face magic without their own powers.

Delia hugged the walls, trying her hardest to stick to the outside of the carnage and make her way towards the secret passageway Dorothy had told her about. Eventually, she reached a painting of an older gentleman draped in what appeared to be royal robes. She reached up and pressed the sash that sat across the man's chest, the painting then swinging inwards into a small opening.

Delia almost had to crawl into the opening as she used the bottom of the frame to swing herself into the room, dropping a small distance to the hard floor.

Delia looked around. The room was only large enough to hold what Delia assumed was the Cryogenic Chamber. The chamber floated on the back wall and other than being suspended in mid-air was a rather underwhelming metal canister. Delia took a deep breath and tried to remember the intricate movements Dorothy had shown her to open the chamber. She closed her eyes to concentrate.

The chamber clicked and a wide door fell open, bathing the space in silver light. Delia grimaced and held a hand up to her eyes, trying to deflect the intensity.

As soon as she heard movement behind her, Delia knew who it was.

"Your friends are losing."

Delia whipped around to face her father. "I don't believe you."

Marcus stepped forward, a look of fake sincerity plastered across his face. "You can stop this, you know. No one else needs to die."

Delia sneers. "Bullshit."

Marcus stepped back, sincerity wiped from his face. "You know what Delia? Contrary to popular belief, I'm not a monster. If your friends surrender, I won't kill them." Marcus paused, a smirk on his face. "I am sorry about your friend. Or girlfriend?"

Delia's eyes widened as she allowed her emotions to take over, snapping her fingers, which resulted in Marcus flying a couple of feet into the air. Delia's hair flew around her face, framing it, as her eyes glazed over. She pushed her hand to the left side of the room and Marcus's limp body followed, but it was as if she was pushing against cement and not air.

As Marcus's body hung by the chamber, Delia repeated the complicated movements from earlier and slowly, Marcus's body went further and further into the chamber.

Delia would always remember her father's face before she closed him in the chamber.

"Goodbye, Dad. I hope you rot."

With a snap of her hands, the silver light from the chamber disappeared and the floating device went back to looking unassuming. Delia felt her legs give out from beneath her and she quickly pushed her hands out to catch her from falling too severely to the ground.

Behind her, Dorothy clambered into the room, clutching a wound on her side.

Delia didn't bother to look behind her, every bone in her body screaming not to move.

"He's gone."

CHAPTER TWENTY-TWO

The sun had just risen as Dorothy stood on the steps of the Emerald City Palace, addressing the Ozians who had gathered. Murmurs rumbled down each street that was full of citizens, each wondering if the Wizard was well and truly gone. Dorothy stood with her head held high, wound around her side bandaged. Delia sat off to the left side of Dorothy, wincing as Lea attended to a large cut down her arm.

Mathias stood out amongst the crowd, mane blowing back and forth in the early morning wind. James stood off to the side of the crowd, a young boy in his arms.

Dorothy waved her hand and her voice echoed around the streets of the Emerald City. "Ozians. It is a great honour to stand in front of you all once more. Marcus Rightfoot is gone."

Dorothy paused as the crowd broke out in applause.

"In time, I will release the details of what happened to me during the years I was not here to serve you. For that, and for what the Wizard's Coalition put you through, I will forever be so sorry. Now, however, is not the time for that information. Now we celebrate the actions, bravery, and heroism of Delia Woodbridge."

Dorothy nodded over to where Delia sat, Lea now next to her after finishing bandaging Delia's wound.

"It is Delia's actions that have saved us all from Marcus's reign. Delia, and Delia alone, should hold the credit for what has been done here today."

Cheers rang out around the crowd, with many a 'thank you' and 'we love you, Delia!' among the easiest to decipher.

"Her actions leading up to and during the removal of Marcus Rightfoot are why I want to offer her the role as my heir. She has showed significant grit and determination, and I know for sure that she has fallen in love with our wonderful country."

Delia's eyes widened comically.

"I hope that she will work beside me to restore Oz and then, once the time is right, succeed me on the throne. I hope you will all respect her and welcome her as you've done for me all these years."

Delia walked alongside Dorothy as they both made their way down one of the busier Emerald City streets. Delia could only watch in awe as Dorothy greeted passers-by like the dignified leader she clearly was. Locals didn't hesitate to approach the pair and thank them for what they had done. As an older Ozian engaged Dorothy in conversations about changing some law, Delia took the chance to take in the city.

It didn't take long before Delia's eyes settled on one building that was looking significantly dilapidated. The front of the house, basically reduced to rubble, spilled onto the street. A couple of plant boxes hung precariously off the side of the building. Delia shook her head as she took it all in, imagining how the citizens had lived in conditions like this for so long.

She waved her hand, and the buildings began to 'stitch' themselves back together. Bricks settled on top of one another and the green hue of the buildings shone once more. Flowers bloomed from the hanging boxes, hues of pinks and yellows standing out amongst the green city.

Any Ozians that had viewed Delia's handy work clapped as the building returned to its former glory.

Dorothy bid goodbye to the older woman and hurried to catch up with Delia, her eyes gleaming at Delia's creation. "Please consider my offer. Talk to your mum and take your time, but I do really think you'd do well here."

Delia smiles.

CHAPTER TWENTY-THREE

Delia studied her mother's face, trying desperately to reconcile the picture of the woman she loved and the woman who had a child with Marcus Rightfoot.

The sun created unusual shadows in the kitchen as they sat across from one another in silence.

"Did you know?"

Delia's mother raised an eyebrow. "Know what?"

Delia sighed and threw her head back in frustration. "That my father was a wizard?"

Tahlia Woodbridge had never felt her heart drop so quickly. Guilt and sadness flooded through her as she desperately tried to scramble together a response to her beloved daughter's question. Tahlia's chair scraped loudly along the kitchen floor as she stood and pottered around the bench, throwing together ingredients for a salad.

"Did you meet him? Marcus?"

Delia sucked in a breath; all of her deepest concerns true in a few quick words. "I thought we told each other everything. I trusted you more than anything. Why wouldn't you tell me this, Mum?"

Tahlia felt her heart break with the simple use of the antonym. Trusted. Past tense. "I was so in love with him. It took me a long time to realise that he was well and truly an evil man. He wanted a family, but I knew I had to end the relationship somehow. Staying with him was becoming dangerous. I stumbled upon what he was going to do, killing his own child…"

Tahlia paused, the memories unwillingly flooding back.

"I faked a miscarriage. I paid a doctor to say that the miscarriage caused too much damage and I would never have biological children. So, he left."

Delia stood and faced her mother, tears threatening to spill. "I'm so sorry…"

"Don't be," she interrupts. "I should have just told you this from the start."

Tahlia grabbed the bowl that she had been throwing salad ingredients into and moved it over to the table. "I spent my whole pregnancy watching my back, scared he'd be back for me, for you."

Delia wiped the tears from her eyes, her anger again replacing her sympathy at her mother's ordeal. "Why are there pictures of me with him? How are there pictures of me with him?"

Tahlia stared out the window, her eyes locked on a bird that flew by. "I was born in Oz, Delia. I ended up here after a portal opened in front of me. I… well? I made those photos. I wanted you to think he was an alright guy because to me, Delia? He was at first. He was the absolute love of my life. To everyone else? He was the epitome of pure evil. I didn't want you to know that, Delia."

Delia's thoughts slowed and her heartbeat wildly in her chest. The silence between mother and daughter was deadly. "Honestly, Mum? I don't know what to say. I'm going to stay with Dorothy for a while. I don't know if I'll be back."

Delia turned from her mother and walked to the door. She refused to let her see the tears on her face.

Tahlia called after her, "Delia! Please! Wait!"

The door slammed in Tahlia Woodbridge's face.

CHAPTER TWENTY-FOUR

The Witch Resistance meeting room was looking a lot brighter since the last time Delia had been there. A new paint job and a duster could go a long way, Dorothy had mused.

Dorothy sat across from Delia at the large table, the only two in the room. "So?"

Delia sighs, her mind still on the conversation with her mother. "I'll stay. I'm not making any promises, though, Dorothy."

Dorothy smiles. "I understand, Delia."

Dorothy could see Delia's mind was elsewhere.

"You saw your mother, didn't you?"

Delia grimaced. "Don't ask."

Dorothy nodded. "When you're ready, yeah?"

Delia smiles.

The Oz fair was so much busier than when Delia had visited with Dorothy—Munsie—all that time ago. Parents walked around with the largest smiles on their faces, letting their kids roam wild and actually be children, a luxury not allowed to them under the rule of Marcus Rightfoot. Dorothy made sure she walked right amongst the crowd, beaming at all the cheerful faces.

James stood at a carnival game with his family, holding his son and chatting to his wife. The occasional person would tap him on the shoulder and ask for a photo. Mathias laughed at a picnic table; his hand wrapped around a beautiful lion.

A stage stood lonely at the corner of the excitement, no one paying the space much attention. This changed after a quick announcement over some loudspeakers, signalling an address from Dorothy. Slowly, the crowds made their way over and soon there was a large audience twittering about. The crowd shushed as they watched Dorothy climb a set of stairs to the stage.

Once more, Dorothy magnified her voice. “Thank you all for being here today. I’m so glad to see so many of you ready to celebrate a new Oz. I’d now like to welcome someone to the stage who has become very important to me both personally and in my fight to rejuvenate Oz.”

Cheers erupted as the Ozians in the audience recognised Delia meekly walking onto the stage, her face covered in a light blush.

Dorothy sent Delia a reassuring smile. “Delia Woodbridge, everyone!”

Once the crowd had quieted down slightly, Dorothy continues, “Now, she’s only staying for a little bit of time, and I hope you will all show her Oz’s vast capability to love. We have many things to discuss but today is one of celebration.”

Dorothy looked back at Delia and gestured her forward. “Delia?”

Delia stepped forward and waved her hands in the pattern Dorothy had done to magnify her voice.

“Hi, everyone. Not so long ago, I was sitting at my desk in a small apartment, dreaming of a different life,” Delia says, chuckling. “Believe me, Oz has been nothing but different. An amazing different, however.”

The crowd let out a round of good-natured laughs, and Delia

continues, "Despite finding the different I dreamed of, I still don't know what my future holds. In fact, I find myself more confused than ever. I believe though, that Oz is the place to provide me with that clarity."

Delia paused and cleared her throat. "I lost someone I really cared for. Andrea Mikaelson believed in Oz with every fibre of her being. I owe her my life and I will never forget her. For her, and for you all, I am dedicating myself to Oz. I want nothing more than to do both Andrea and Dorothy proud, and I want nothing short of complete and utter happiness for the citizens of Oz." Delia felt herself choke up. "So thank you, Oz, for showing me it's okay to feel a little lost."

ACKNOWLEDGMENTS

I would write short stories in school and never finish them, always having to provide a cliff hanger so I could hand them up to the teacher. To actually have a finished novel blows my mind, and I know that the little girl who struggled to tame her imagination would be just as shocked.

Thank you to Matthew Broughton for bringing Oz to life so vividly.

Thank you to Annie Booker for making my writing legible.

Thank you to all my enemies, who provided me with enough ammunition to prove them wrong. I hope you see my book and eat your words.

This is for the little girl that would lose so much time to the worlds in her books. Who found so much solace and so much happiness. This is for that girl that got told she read too much but kept reading anyway. Never again will that little girl be told off for reading her book because everyone deserves to do something they love. (And everyone knows that little girl ended up smarter than the other kids)

Thank you to my Dorothy, my Nanna, for doing nothing but allowing my love of books to flourish. You are the reason I became such a big reader.

Thank you to my Mum, my Tahlia, for being my best friend. For being the reason that I'm still here to write this book. I'll try to not resent the fact that you don't have secret Ozian ancestry.

And thank you to my readers. You've really made my dreams come true. Thanks for having faith in little old me. Just know that you will find your way one day, and it's okay to not have all the answers.

I've learnt a lot between first writing this and now (In 2025). It's been a really long road and I'm so thankful to all the people that have welcomed me into the writing community.

I mainly want to thank Tara Jean for looking back through Oz and giving it a "fresh coat" of paint. Not only did she make me feel better about grammar issues in the first edition , but she inspired me to keep going.

I also want to thank Jennah from Flutterby Formatting for giving Oz a professional look.

Lastly , I want to thank Mickey, my inspiration for Munsie and Delia's "Earth" cat, Mick. I love you so much and my heart hurts every day you're not here. Thank you for being the best animal sidekick I could ever have wanted.

ABOUT THE AUTHOR

Hope Swan is a fantasy author from South Australia, Australia. Her first book, Oz, was published in 2024, after her university project turned into something more and she realises her dream of being an author. Hope's books will always have drama, sass, and at least one incredibly sarcastic character that she knows you'll love!

When she's not writing, Hope loves to dance, go to the gym, and put her film degree to good use on movie night!

Watch out for Hope's second NA fantasy novel Oz: One Wizard's Carnage (set for release in 2025) and the prequel, Althie, (Wicked fans unite!) about the infamus Wicked Witch of the West.

Join Hope on Instagram @hopeauthorofficial

ALSO BY HOPE SWAN

Coming soon

Oz Four

The Clean

An Anthology

www.ingramcontent.com/pod-product-compliance
Lightning Source LLC
Chambersburg PA
CBHW060622310726
48982CB00003B/647
9780646890890